10 FOR EVERYTHING
REDUX

10
FOR
EVERYTHING

REDUX

A COLLECTION OF
STORIES AND POEMS

RACHEL KANN

tangerine
tide

Published by
Tangerine Tide
An imprint of
Orange Ocean Press
PO Box 931573
LA, CA 90093

do it all the time uses lyrics from
Kiss Off by the Violent Femmes,
from their eponymous album, *Violent Femmes*; 1982,
written by Gordon Gano.
the way back uses lyrics from
Scenario by A Tribe Called Quest,
from their album *The Low End Theory*; 1991,
written by Ali Shaheed Muhammad,
Malik Taylor, and Trevor Tahiem Smith.

ISBN: 978-1-885021-08-3
Printed in the United States of America
Second Edition, Reprint
June 2013
Copyright 2013 by Rachel Kann

ACKNOWLEDGEMENTS

**Thanks to the following publications in which
the poems and stories below previously appeared:**

Automatic Lighthouse UK: special, this precise desire
Beyond the VCP: word to the why?s
Blue Arc West: free, fall
Coachella Review: daiyenu
getunderground: 12 days, meantime, parts, and this...
GW Review: come
Her Mark: 4:39 a.m.
His Rib: badland between
Into The Blue: chosen
Kotori Magazine: disappearing
loudmouth: montaña de oro
MediaCake: wesley
A Poets' Haggadah: daiyenu
Praxis: my mother built me out of sticks
Quiddity: my mother built me out of sticks
Schuykill Valley Journal: lie down beside you
SGVPQ: lucky, maybe, when the light went out
So Luminous the Wildflowers: pretty talk
Sou'Wester: tumble
Word Warriors: montaña de oro, titular

THANKS TO G. MURRAY THOMAS
AT ORANGE OCEAN PRESS

Never more the cries of unsatisfied love be absent from me,
Never again leave me to be the peaceful child I was
before what there,
in the night,
By the sea, under the yellow and sagging moon,
The messenger there arous'd—the fire, the sweet hell within,
The unknown want, the destiny of me.
Walt Whitman
Out of Cradle Endlessly Rocking

I'm one of those regular weird people.
Janis Joplin

I guess what everyone wants more than anything else is to be
loved.
Ella Fitzgerald

One may have a blazing hearth in one's soul, and yet no one ever
comes to sit by it.
Vincent van Gogh

Ain't never been no nothin' like me.
Muhammad Ali

CONTENTS

STORIES

DISAPPEARING

You need some old-school juju. Some Houdini shit. Pre-Houdini shit. Hell, pre-magick-with-a-k type shit. Some shit in Aramaic. You need to poof...disappear. And tonight, as you lose your shit in Frank's bathroom, you may not be Catholic, but your god sure as hell is. You are bent over the dirtyish porcelain, puking your guts out.

Except that you aren't really, you're just pretending to. You are a master of illusion. More often than not, you find yourself mid-hoax before you've even consciously decided to go through with it. So you're retching and whimpering, pouring a glass of water in the toilet for that extra splash of truth. You are pray-conjuring for a knock on the door, which finally comes.

"Nita, Nita, seriously, you're freaking me out. Are you ok?"

"I'm fucking aces", you warble, trying to sound as martyrish as humanly possible. You want him to see how much this is tearing you apart.

***

Two nights earlier, it's whiskey night at Lily's house, and she's just picked up this tripped-out book at Goodwill. It's called, like, *Crazy Fucking Facts That Will Make You Super Nauseous* or something like that. You read this shit about Freud. You learn something foul: He had cancer in his mouth-face-cheek area toward the end of his life.

Here's what's gnarly: his shit was like, rotting off. So his private practice dwindled away. Because the stench was so unbearable. People, specifically patients, could not bear to be in the same room. With him. That's brutal. Poor Freud. Poor Freud with his vagina dentata and hysterical blindness and Electra complex. All the girls pinching their collective nose as they backed out of his office for the very last time.

You go back to your place and fall asleep fast. This is what you instantly dream: You are back home. Home home. Not that you belong anywhere. But you are hometown-home. Going around like everything is fine, and then you start to have this pain in your gums. It is a really bad, black pain. You are with your mom. She is sorrowful but calm and she says,

"Nita, honey, this is hard to say. Terribly hard."

"What, momma?"

"Oh, honey, you're dead. You've been dead for a while now. You're starting to decompose."

And she guides your shoulders to the mirror and shows you how your skull, a lot of it, is showing through the side of your face.

"When you get to the next place, you will be whole again. It's time to go. It's time to go."

So you step outside, and suddenly you are in the middle of the meadow in Central Park, and it is that perfect kind of day where the breeze barely feels like anything, that's how right the temperature is. And mom is long gone.

You are surrounded by beautiful men in pastels, sweaters tied jauntily over their shoulders. You find your circle of gay-

2

postles. Each of them already has a dead person to carry to heaven. Only this Saint Petery-Jesusy guy is left.

He seems like the leader, obviously. Too busy-important to be of assistance. You flood with the familiar poison of feeling awkward and out of place. Like, fuck, even in the afterlife you are the fifth wheel. But then, Saint Peter dude calls you over.

"Nita, what are you looking for? I am right here, waiting for you."

And with that, you curl yourself into his sixty-five-year-old-man-in-Banana Republic-pants lap, stare up at his Lacoste shirt the color and texture of peach fuzz.

And he says, "Now you are here. With us. We were waiting. For you. Now we can go."

And you all float up to the sky, like a supernatural pride march, Bronski Beat softly lilting all around.

When you wake, you run to the mirror to see if there is skull showing. But you are intact, you are alive, you are whole. Which is good. For now. You guess. It must have been the Freud racket, combined with some second-rate *Sixth Sense* symbolism for cheap measure. Plus you ate left over Pad Woon Sen just before you went to bed. So you chalk it up to all that.

That afternoon, your blood turns to tar when you talk to Frank. You call him from the celly, on speakerphone, sitting in traffic moving like taffy. He answers, finally, for the first time in a few days.

"Nita, hey. Hey Neaty, listen."

"Hi Frank."

Breath. Breathing.

"Nita, I, something's happened. Something bad. Really bad. I need to be by myself."

"Wait, what? Why, what?"

"Something's happened. To me. I've changed. I have a problem. Nita, I can't do this anymore."

"Whatever's happened, we can work through it. Let me love you through it."

"No, Nita. I have something very wrong with me. I have a

hole in me. It's bad. A hole. Right in my cheek."

Your legs go numb, like when you drive by a cop and the adrenaline floods. You grip the steering wheel 'til your knuckles crack. You know you haven't told him about the dream. Or the Freud thing. The world wavers sideways through the windshield. You are silent. What would Frank make of your mouth opening and closing like a fish death in slow motion?

"Nita, this isn't easy. It's bigger than a quarter, and it's getting bigger every day, and I hate myself, I loathe myself, I feel like a monster. And I can't put off dealing with this. I have to fix this."

"But, but, I love you. I don't care."

"Yeah see, that's exactly it. You. Don't. Care."

"Frank! That's not fair! You know what I mean. I mean that I accept your flaws. I embrace your flaws. I want to help you. I don't care if you have flaws. I can help you. I will help you. Let me help you. We can fix this together. Please don't fucking shut me out"

"Nita. It's over. This is something I have to do on my own. This hole in me is what's standing between us." You know this is a lie. You can predict all of this. You know right then that you should hang up. There are sleights of hand all around.

"Frank. Please don't say that. Please don't say that if it's not true."

"This IS the truth."

"So then, when you are all better, that means we are all better too?" A pause. A too-long pause. A long-enough-for-your-heart-to-crumple-like-a-beer can-against-a-frat boy's-head pause. Fuck. FUCK.

"Nita. What do you want from me? I'm falling apart. Quite literally. I can't promise you that. I can't promise you anything. I don't know anything. I don't know who I am anymore. And I don't know who I will be when I am a whole again. I respect you too much to make empty promises."

"Respect? Respect? But you don't respect me enough to give me the truth." The truth is that you don't matter to him. He doesn't love you. You know if he did, it wouldn't matter if half his head fell off. It wouldn't make him push you away. He would want to be near you. The truth is that even whole, you are inadequate. You are never enough. Not skinny enough, not pretty enough, not

4

smart enough, not good enough. Everyone you know goes away in the end. There's something wrong with you. What comes out is, "I am flawed. I am evil. I am cursed. I'm the monster. Not you. They always walk away. You are fucking walking away. You're leaving me alone when you promised you wouldn't."

"I'm gonna go now, Nita."

"I love you, please, you made me believe. Frank. You gave me hope. You made me think I might not die alone in a pool of my own piss and despair, a bitch without the balls for suicide, dying sixty years too late. I want to thank you for that."

"NITA." Frank is really yelling now. Really mad. "I'm hanging UP. I have to deal with this on my own terms. This is my hole to fix."

"Ok. Hang up then. Hang up."

And Frank does, and you are really choking. Super sobbing. Crying in a crazy psycho Greek Tragedy way. And, thank god, the traffic has picked up to the texture of Cool Whip, at least. Because it's all coming out. You are screaming and moaning and even forming words, mostly "I can't...I can't...oh god oh god, I can't. I can't." You are having one of those *this is for it all, since the beginning*, from the bottom of your feet weep sessions.

It's good to be in the car. You couldn't go off like this at your shitty apartment. The whole building, and probably block, would hear you. You suspect that even in the middle of some naturey setting, you couldn't really cut loose like this. You'd still fear somebody catching wind. No, in motion, propelling forward, in the bubble of your shitty Honda, this is the only way to do it.

***

Here's the thing. Here's where you were at before Frank. He saw you in the library, while you were waiting for a computer to get on the internet. You were desperate to check your email, just in case David Blaine had emailed you back. You had offered to be his lovely assistant. You had a friend in the business who stole his email address for you. You really felt like this might be the thing that broke through, put you in direct contact.

You smelled Frank before you saw him. Cool Water cologne. It was your tacky high school throwback Achilles heel. It was chemical, you couldn't help it. He sat down right next to you, and you were stiff as morning wood through the neck.

You turned to look, and he was all kinds of cholo. Like, straight gangster. Wifebeater. Khakis. Shaved head. Moustache. A neck tattoo that read "Sad Eyes". He was terrifying, and beautiful, and smelled faintly of b.o. under the Cool Water smell. He looked right at you, eyes pure as Buddha.

"Let me take you out." He said it without a hint of agenda.

You were stymied. "Like take me out? Like on a date?"

"U huh."

"No. No no no."

"Can I just ask why?"

"Because. Because I'm like this. Because…I'm all wacked out. I'm all fucked up. I'm here to see if fucking David Blaine has emailed me. Shit is incredibly fucking really real. Do you need this mess?"

Frank just blinked his beautiful frog-like and guileless eyes, and said, "I don't even know who David Blaines is. So… Friday night? Saturday?"

And then the weird guy with one giant dreadlock that hung all the way down his back finally finished on station number fourteen. He got up, and so that basically meant your internet time was ticking away. You stood up and walked over to your computer. You sat down and did not turn around, just logged into your Yahoo account. Two minutes later, you smelled his approach like an amen. He didn't say a word, just slipped his caramel hand sidelong of your keyboard. When you looked, he was gone. But he left a Halls cough drop wrapper there, with his phone number scrawled across it.

That Saturday night, he gave you sangria. With bits of apple and orange that you fingered right out of the glass and into your mouth. He had a Volkswagen the exact off-white color of chewed-up Doublemint gum. He knew some magic. Real stuff, not some David Blaine shit. Santeria, like, spells and stuff. He told you about how his grandmother had seen things, things other people couldn't see, and how she'd died from falling off a really high roof, and nobody knew if she had killed herself or been pushed. Either way, she died from knowing too much.

And he also told you about his lezzie sister, which you loved. And his passionate mother who cried all the time, and his father the painter.

And he took you in his room and showed you some pictures on his laptop, of graf art he had done. And they were really good, and you could feel the inside of you unzipping. And then you went outside with him and the sangria and sat on the dirty stairs and looked at the slutty wonderful moon.

It was like when you think someone is super hot and they do something really assholey and you watch their hotness slide off like a silk robe. Watch them instantly uglify. Just like that, but in reverse. People had definitely grown on you before. Slowly though. Super slow. Slowly rearranged in your head and become attractive in their worth-it-ness. Like a Seurat painting that you had to back away from to see the big picture. But this was quick. This was over. You were sprung.

You just turned and kissed him. It felt like all the nonsense turning into psalms. All the sandpaper loneliness melting to velvet redemption. You were gone.

You went right in his bedroom without batting an eyelash. You knew you were gonna. Fuck your dignity, fuck propriety, fuck him. Fuck the shit out of him. And you fell with him, to the futon that was on the floor. And he smelled like home, wherever that was. And the kisses and the hands and the legs pressed into you like paradise.

But he couldn't get it up.

"Nita, I, I'm sorry. I'm embarrassed. This never happens." His words echoed like every cliché ever. Bounced off the particleboard walls. And so you said all the cliché stuff back.

"It's ok, seriously, you make me feel so good. Don't worry about it, the more you worry about it, the bigger deal it becomes, and then..."

"I know, Nita, it's cool. Thanks"

You slept naked in his arms all night. It was like returning, except when you were fitful, panicked, wondering what was so unappealing about you that Frank couldn't pop a chub. You remembered how you were an outcaste, a monster, destined to die alone, and figured that you had tricked the system somehow. In the back of your skull, a faint filmstrip clicked to life and started up again. It shows all the times you give your power away. It was adding the footage of Frank to the master.

You woke up and you'd started your period in his bed. It could've been worse, it wasn't like "Carrie", could've been way worse, but still. Crazy. Raw earth.

***

And you'd fallen into each other like that as days smeared into weeks and then months. Until this.

After the phone call, after you cry your country song eyes out in the car, after the wave rolls through, after you non-hysterically and methodically and really quite calmly - if you do say so yourself, which you do - remove his number from your cell phone, he calls you back.

"Hey." Frank is hoarse. "Hey, I just wanted you to know that I'm sorry if I yelled at you, I didn't mean to, and I appreciate you too, and you are incredible and beautiful and I am so grateful, and I just, yeah, I just wanted you to know that. Ok?"

You are already a million miles away.

"Kay. Thanks. Cool." Your heart is frostbitten. Fuck him for making you let your walls down for no reason. Fuck that.

"Nita. Can you just come over? Can we just talk about it?" And then it flips, because that's exactly what you want to do. So you do. And then you get there, and it flops, everything's happening too fast, and he clearly doesn't love you anymore, if he ever did. He's turned away, hunched in the dark, won't let you near the hole, the disappearing part. Won't even let you near any part of him. And you are silently dreaming of the magic that you bet Saint Jude could do for you. And you lock yourself in the bathroom.

Frank has the opposite idea of what terrifies you.

DO IT ALL THE TIME.

RESPECTFULLY:
AFTER LEA DESCHENES AND BEFORE HER, GORDON GANO

One: 'cause you left me

Hey, wanna know the latest? My current scam is to get involved with someone and force her to keep it secret. Really make it stressful. Any reason but cheating, that's too easy. You know, something to keep the bitch just a little bit on her toes. Let her worry I'm ashamed of her, ashamed of people knowing we're together.

The more insecure a girl is, the more tail you get. Saves you a grip of loot, an unexpected side benefit. Didn't think of that before I started, but it makes sense. This isn't pretty, it's just truth.

See Cait? Upshot, no fucking female is going to pull the rug out from under me. Not ever again.

Two: for my family

Donya is perfect. She's got more issues than a medical library. Hates her body, thinks she's ugly and stupid, massive

9

abandonment hang-ups.

Always seeking approval, which means she looks smoking hot twenty-four seven, decked to the nines, trying too hard, attempting to make it seem effortless.

She could suck the chrome off a tailpipe and I can bend her like a pretzel. Crazy bitches are always the best in bed. Everyone knows that. You know that, Cait.

You'd love this: I told her that the reason we have to keep it under wraps is that my mother, who's deathly sick, is living with me. That if she found out I was dating someone ethnic, it would kill her. Quite literally.

Poor Donya. I don't even know what the hell breed she is so I didn't specify. She didn't question it. She ate it up, hook, line, and sinker. Hates herself that much.

Three: for my heartache

And what force conspired to amalgamate all these physical and mental qualities and quirks into one teeny tiny fragile package, Cait? I'll give you one guess.

I'd like to personally thank Sasha or Sergei or whatever fucking enterprising Russian brought ballet to the US of A. I'd like to shake his hand. This shit will fuck babygirl up faster than playing hide the sausage with Uncle Chester. And keep her in better shape, too. But I don't need to tell you that.

Four: for my headache

Everything happened out of order with you, Cait. Everything.

We were partying at my place junior year. My mom was out of town visiting her internet perv boyfriend, like she was for pretty much all of high school.

Nine or ten of us. We were drinking SoCo mixed with Sunkist soda and smoking pot out of the empty can. You were there with Natty, and she was trying to get with Brian.

I watched you get more and more tired and fucked up. You grabbed Natty and begged her to take off with you. But she was on a mission, there was no chance. I watched you sneak upstairs to go crash out in my bed until she was done. On your way, you told her what you were up to, and made her promise to come and get you before she left. I heard the whole thing.

I was sitting at the dinner table. The kitchen was spinning. I was thinking how I'd better drink some water before I passed out, because the jackhammers were already starting in my skull.

Five: for my lonely
Donya and I went to the Christmas party together at work. She waits tables at the restaurant with me. I told her nobody there could know we were together. I told her I didn't want those fucks all up in our business. That I didn't shit where I ate, thank you very much.

I spent the better part of the night chain smoking by the pool table, seething. Donya looked drop-dead. Dudes were hitting on her. Hard. And while she wasn't flirting back, she wasn't telling them to fuck off either. Chris, the manager who always reeks of Fahrenheit, was wearing this silky blue shirt, and had her cornered.

I wanted to beat the shit out of him.

But, see, I'd tied my own hands. I couldn't say dick.

Six: for my sorrow
I'd watched your perfect ass stumble upstairs. Watched you go in my bedroom and close the door behind you. I thought about how me and you and Natty would drive around listening to The Femmes with the heater on full blast and all the windows rolled down. I'd never thought about that before.

I realized I was all alone in the kitchen with my spins, everybody was hooking up. Natty and Brian were in the yard macking, I could see them through the window. I felt myself flush with anger and wanting. I felt in the way, out of place in my own goddamned house.

I cracked open my door and silently climbed into my bed, spooned you from behind. You were out cold, and nuzzled your dancer's ass into me. I put my hands on your lower back. Nothing. Reached inside your underwear, your flesh was colder than I expected. You didn't resist. Who the fuck were you dreaming of? I slipped my fingers down and then up, inside your pussy.

Seven: no tomorrow
I moved two of them, in and out, slowly and gently, and you were getting wet. You were a slut in your sleep, bucking and

moaning. When you snapped awake, you gasped, didn't say a word. Scrambled up out of the bed, straightened your sleep-crumpled clothes, and stumbled out the door, calling for Natty.

I stared at the ceiling with my dick in my hand. By the time I went back into the kitchen, you and Natty were gone, and I knew you had told her what happened. You never spoke to me again, unless it was absolutely necessary. Like when it would have made more of a scene to not speak to me.

Eight: i forget what eight was for
Donya doesn't mean shit. Nobody does. Nobody gets in now. Nobody touches me. Not really. I get laid, I laugh at these sluts, but every pussy I touch is yours. Every ass I spoon around is yours. Every back walking out the door in silence belongs to you.

Nine: for a lost god
Cait, after you left the party, it was like I snagged inside you. I have been unraveling ever since. You never confronted me. Neither did Natty. She was kinda distant for like a week, but then we kept right on kicking it like nothing happened.

Drove past the fields of lettuce screaming with the tape player, wondering why we couldn't get just one kiss, just one fuck, never acknowledging that you weren't there, or why. I hated Natty for staying friends with me and not sticking up for you.

I fucking hate chicks. I don't get them. Why did you stay friends with her when you knew she was still cool with me?

The farther away you walk, the more I come apart. You're still pulling me to pieces. Cait, I will be in love with you until the day I die. You took that part of me with you. I will die like this, a pile of shapeless unstrung nothing.

Ten: ten ten ten for everything
Everything.
Everything.
Everything.

THE HISTORIAN

It's not easy being me. I have always been me.
But I can't even remember just when I comprehended what being
me meant. It's a heavy load and it was a gradual realization.

I've spent most of my life searching people's faces for
some recognition, some understanding, someone like me. But
that seems less and less likely with every passing day.

It's easy, when you're young, to go from "My! Isn't he
bright!" at three, to thinking that learning is just easier for you
at ten. And then to a smugly superior streak as knowledge just
seems to flow into by the time you're fourteen. And here I am,
now, at nineteen. Having realized what the deal is. Trying to cope
with being the historian. Failing miserably.

There are those of us who…what we do is…wow, this is
hard. Ok. Who, through no conscious intent of our own, create
reality. Through our thoughts. I am not being pretentious here,
and I would do anything to change it. Believe me, I've tried. It's
not like I have the power to make things how I want them to

be. It's more like, this passing thought will come through my head? You know? And then I know it's going to be one of those things. Random things. Like maybe you will see on the news that they found a new ancient text written in a heretofore-unknown language. That kind of stuff, that's me. A girl who's been missing since she was eight found in a ravine. A lost John Lennon studio recording surfaces. Et Cetera. And that stuff is actually mostly cool. But just as often, it's really not cool. At all.

And it's not always newsworthy stuff either. It's my stuff. Mostly, it's been almost impossible to even seriously date at all because I was always seeing her cheat on me. Or even just seeing how it was all gonna play out in the end. I didn't want to go through it, you know? But sometimes I don't make anything happen much at all for a while. Like I said, I have no control over which thoughts will be fruitful. Or whatever. And it's never about "force of nature" stuff or anything like that. Crazy weather, et cetera. It's always human.

My first really strange memory is the Janis Joplin thing. I was seven. I had a poster of her in my room. Curled and finger print smeared on the black border with pushpins in the corners. The night before she died, I was sitting in there with my mom, who stared out the window at the brown fence and the late twilight warmth. She sighed.

"Isn't it nice here, Noa?"

"'Bye, Janis." It came out of no place inside me. I reached up in one swift motion and ripped Janis off the wall. The pushpins popped out on all but one corner, which tore and stayed attached to the wall, a chunk of grimy black paper. Another one bounced off my nose before falling to the yellow yarn rug.

"What the hell? Noa, what on earth are you doing?"

"I'm saying goodbye." I turned around to face her. Crumpled the poster up, and dropped it in the tin oval of trash can.

"Well. I, honey are you ok? I'm going to check on the meatloaf." And that was the last we spoke of that. The next night, I was making a Lego spaceship in the living room while mom watched the news from the couch. The reporter said that Janis Joplin had died, and I heard the strangest sound of sucking in air from behind me. I turned to look at my mother. She hopped up and said she had to go see how the tuna casserole was coming along. I snuck to the edge of the kitchen but stayed around the corner, stared at the circular brown and orange patterns in the linoleum and listened to my mom's hushed and panicked phone voice, uttering to her sister in a stage whisper.

The fear in her eyes was like a stain she could never quite wash out. That was how I first learned that what was inside me was powerful. And that power was scary. I would try to comfort mom by sharing happy stuff with her. I could tell her who would win the lottery sometimes, but it wasn't like I could ever make her win, of course. But then the good stuff would scare her just as much.

I ultimately settled on getting really impeccable grades. That made her smile. I locked everything else up inside. We talked around the issue, never about it. Mom really wanted to figure out what was going on with me. She'd read Oliver Sacks and stuff. Wanted to treat it like a brain illness.

I was terrified that if anybody found out what I had been doing, especially a scientist or doctor, I'd be locked up forever, given a lobotomy, kept like a monster in a cage, killed, something really bad. I was terrified that that was exactly what should be done with someone like me. I was also terrified of being alone and keeping it all secret inside me.

I've been studied. Had these weird electrodes stuck to my skull when I was fifteen, and they kept me in this pseudo-bedroom for twenty-four hours of surveillance. Watched me sleep through a one-way mirror and videotaped it too.

"Just relax, try to sleep. That's what we need to see, your sleeping brain. See its waves, cool?" The guy in scrubs smiled, but I was creeped out. He looked too young to be a doctor.

"Are you an MD?" I leveled him as best I could.

"Haha, nope. Just a lab tech. I'm qualified though, don't worry."

"Great. So, I'm never going to be able to sleep in here without some meds." I meant this.

"No can do. We gotta see those brain waves all natural style."

"If it's just because you're not a doctor, we can call my mom and she can tell you I am allowed to take them and I really can't sleep without them."

"Sorry, bro."

I laid down in the crappy fake bed in the crappy fake bedroom and felt like I'd never fall asleep. But in the morning, I woke up, so I must have. I felt tricked and disoriented, angry at my mom who was waiting in the lobby when they let me out the next morning. The sun was glaring in my eyes and I felt dirty and sticky. They made us wait there while the neurologist read the results like a lie-detector test printout.

When they called out "Calhoun? Noa?" we walked to the back, into his office. He was smiling his wrinkly eyes and folding and unfolding his hands. He said the results were inconclusive and he really couldn't help us. My mother stared at him like he just told her Santa raped the tooth fairy.

"What do you mean, inconclusive? What couldn't you conclude?"

"I'm sorry Miss Calhoun, I-"

"It's Ms." Mom was on her whole liberated thing.

"Ms. Calhoun. Sorry. Right. Yes. Ms. Calhoun." His hands opened and closed like a venus flytrap. "Ms. Calhoun, unfortunately, I don't know what to do for your son at this point. The test results did not give us any information that we would have needed."

My mom was shaking, and stood up in her high heeled sandals with the bows on the toes. "Dr. Pratt, this is simply not acceptable to me." I could tell by the weird propriety in her choice of words that something was coming apart inside of her. "I took out a second mortgage on my home to do these tests."

"Perhaps, Ms. Calhoun, if you could tell us what symptoms are causing your concern with Noa, I would have more of direction to go in. I warned you that this would likely happen." She wanted to tell Dr. Pratt. She wanted to more than anything. But she couldn't. I had agreed to let her take me to get poked and prodded, but only after she swore to never say what she had seen from me. What she'd heard. "Noa," Dr Pratt continued, "tells me he is fine."

"Noa, let's go." She spoke through the smallest hole she could make her lips into. I watched her eyeballs turn from white to bright pink, and I followed her out to the orange Vanagon. As we drove back to the house, I stared at the fat tears rolling down her cheek, which she never wiped away.

Two weeks later I saw her feet dangling above the garage floor forty-five minutes before I rode up. I left my bicycle in the middle of the street and ran in, to her.

I sat in there on the ground, backpack still on, next to her pantyhosed lifeless limbs until the police came in the next day.

That's when I went to live in the hospital for a while. They said they wanted to "observe" me. My doctor was so beautiful that I was hard all day almost. She was so beautiful that I almost told her the truth. I mean, all of it. She was like a colt, strong limbed and proud across the collarbone, with shiny brown hair that hung down her back. Doctor E. Her name was Eunice Wainworth, but she hated being called Eunice, and felt like last names were too proper. "Makes me feel old, Noa" she'd say, rolling her eyes.

And sometimes I would just call her E. And I would also think...*But you are old. Like, compared to me, you...are...old. Old and beautiful. You are the most beautiful thing I have ever seen.* That part was all inside my head, not out loud. Until one day, it was out loud. We were sitting outside, on the chipped green bench. She was making some comparison between the falling leaves and my mom's death. She was trying to be helpful. It was cold outside.

"Soon the snow will fall..." she trailed off.

"Thanks, E." She furrowed her brows at me. She did that when I left the "Doctor" part out. But she let me do it. "It's cold already," I continued. "It's cold." I moved closer to her on the bench, felt her stiffen.

"Noa, one of these days, you're going to have to tell us what you were being tested for. I know you're only fifteen, you've had to grow up fast. It's horrible what you've been through. Sometimes life isn't fair, or doesn't make a whole lot of sense. It may not be fair. But now, there's just you, and only you know what is going on with you. We want to help you. Can't you just let us help?"

My mother's ankles hung before my eyes. And I saw piles and piles of dead bodies suddenly. Hundreds. Babies. Everything. I knew it was real. And I started shaking. Because I had made it happen. Someplace south, and green.

"Noa," Doctor E said. "Noa".

And in that moment, I felt powerless. And I felt like maybe I could let the weight lift off my shoulders, if what I was starting to see about myself was really turning out to be true. And I wanted to plant it inside Doctor Eunice Wainworth. Let her take care of me. Let her fix me, I wanted to believe she was like me. That she was cursed with the same um, abilities. But I wasn't ready to say it out loud. Because I still couldn't make it real by giving name to it.

So, faced with that non-option, I went with plan b. Because she looked into my eyes like something real. Because when I looked in her eyes, just right into them, I couldn't see the future to create a past. It all somersaulted into a nothing-blur. So I told her everything else, the stuff bottlenecked on top of the deeper stuff. Told her how beautiful she was, that I didn't care how old she was, that I wished she didn't either, that when I was around her I was frozen inside a moment, that I wanted to get the fuck out of the hospital for exactly that reason, and, for exactly that reason, I never wanted to leave.

I certainly didn't tell her about the Jonestown thing.

She stared at me, and I could feel the tears burning trails down my frozen face, just like my mother's; unattended to.

The next day, Doctor E talked to me in only fake happy. She had "found a placement" for me. It was decided that I would go live with my aunt and do outpatient. New doctor, fresh start, no more hospital. I didn't even try to fight it.

It's weird how different those of us with a forced perspective act when we're still like, kids, like, not considered adults. Those of us who slip out of the life-and-death level melodrama of adolescence. It's always a violation. My brain was not my own, plus, my secret grew like slow morning sickness inside me.

My aunt was whatever. I never really knew her, and now, she seemed scared of me. I didn't want to talk to her, didn't want to know what she knew, didn't want to discuss anything with her.

This one time, I had stayed at her house when I was nine. Her very rich-ass house. I was making a model airplane and went pee. On my way back into the living room, I stepped on the tube of model airplane glue. It squirted out in a clear squiggle blob in the middle of the cream colored carpet. I panicked and put the model airplane box on top of it and went to bed.

The next day, when she asked me about it, I played dumb. She sent me home. Sent my mom a note written in terse cursive along with me. I read it all on the train, about how I was a liar, and maybe had sociopathic tendencies, all the ways my mom was raising me wrong. And how I used to seem like such a happy little guy, and how that was the way she was going to choose to remember me, not as this evil pre-teen.

Now that I was a sophomore, motherless, out of ideas, I was polite enough to her. I mean, come on, she took me in. I did all my damn "please"s and "thank you"s, but I planned to get emancipated as soon as possible. Aside from running in the kitchen with a towel the moment before she accidentally lobbed off the tip of her thumb while chopping carrots, I kept the historian stuff well hidden away from her. Besides, that cut was bleeding so bad that she was just glad to have something to wrap it up with.

I started at the new high school. It was all a surreal blur, none of it mattered to me anymore. I slipped from Pre-Calc to some godforsaken class called Math C in about two months. We literally would do things like mazes and word jumbles. That was our math work. Sometimes we would practice more applicable things, I guess. Like, how to fill out personal checks.

The class was full of stoners and dumb hot chicks. I actually saw a fist fight in that class over a can of Skoal, which the stoners would stick in their lip. When they had to spit, they'd do it right on the floor when our senile teacher, Mr. Kagan, was spacing out. I saw a guy piss right out the back door of that classroom once.

I never got emancipated. Never made any real friends at that school. I just skated through and barely graduated. Stayed as numb and invisible as possible. Barely breathed. And then I moved to the city, and that's where I met Jenny. I was working in a Kinko's, graveyard shift. She came in at three a.m.

"Hey, Noa" She said, eyes darting to my nametag and

back to my face. "Are you super busy?"

She had bad breath and eye boogers, and her ponytail was haggard with a halo of frizz around it. She wore a sweatshirt that she had obviously wiped some snot on. I really thought she was beautiful. I could picture her after a shower. Graveyard at Kinko's really brought out the truth of people. Like the real deal shit. I could see that even with all that she was beautiful.

I still had to cop my Kinko's attitude.

"I'm pretty busy, yeah, what can I do you for?"

She laughed. "Do me? Anyway..."

I played it straight deadpan and felt the buckles inside me tighten. The straps around my guts and heart strain. It was all flooding into me, and I didn't want to see it, but this time it seemed good. I was seeing good.

She slapped a piece of wrinkled paper down on the counter. It was folded in quarters and each fourth had a hand written flyer in it. There were also some cut out words gluesticked on there, a'la ransom note style or something.

"I need to make four hundred of these, hot pink. That's not the hard part. I can do that. But your paper cutters suck. I need to know that you will cut these for me in that machine thingey that cuts them all at once. Before I make the copies. See, I'm a planner..."

Right, I'm thinking. *That's why you need to make these at 3:07 a.m.*

"...and I don't like to be taken by surprise. So I need that commitment from you. And also, I am totally willing to pay for that, but I don't want to pay the additional setup fee you guys charge. That's just not cool. That shit hurts my feelings. And if you're not able to pony up your piece of the deal for any part of this bargain, that's fine. Just let me know now. Like I said, I just don't like surprises."

I felt like I was slipping down a tube, like the inside of one of those weird water wiener things. That rubber toy filled with liquid that just slides and slides through your hands, no matter how hard you hold on to it. I couldn't see anything good, but I wasn't seeing any of the bad stuff either. I was searching my instant daydreams of this crusty girl in my mind. No cheating, no thrown plates, no slammed doors.

But something felt so helpless, so wrong. But the helpless part also felt so inevitable. And that felt. Well, it felt kinda freeing too.

And I already was wanting to pour all my secrets inside of her. I wanted to throw her in a shower. I wanted to watch her masturbate under the running water. And then I wanted to pull her hand away and show her that I already knew how she liked it. And make her come until she begged me to stop, and not stop.

And when she started crying I would still keep going, and after she came three times more than she thought was possible, she would fall asleep on my chest, and never tell her friends about it, even the ones she told everything, because they wouldn't understand the part where I wouldn't stop, and she'd feel ashamed of not knowing how to explain it right.

"Yeah, uh..."

"Jenny"

"yeah Jenny."

"Yeah what?"

"Yeah, I can do that for you. I can cut them for you."

"Thanks." She turned on her heel and ran off the copies after I handed her some hot pink 8 1/2 by 11. I offered her cardstock, but she said no. I wouldn't have charged her extra.

I watched her every second, just stood there frozen and waited for her to finish. She walked back over and plunked them down in front of me.

"You're kind of, different, Noa."

"Um, ok." I looked down and read the flyers. They weren't advertising anything. There was no punk gig, no poetry reading, no political rally. They said,

> this is really happening, all of it, get ready. the sooner you believe, the sooner the changes can come. and come. and come.

"You know what Jenny? You're kind of weird too."

"I didn't say weird, Noa, I said different." But my back was already to her, I walked over to the cutter and quickly sliced the stack in half, placed one half on top of the other, and halved them again. I grabbed some rubber bands and began bundling them into chunks.

"I can help you with that." I brought them over to the

customer counter and we rubber banded them together, in silence for a moment. Then,

"So, what are you using these for, Jenny?"

"Ugh, um, I don't feel like I can explain it. Put it this way: I just want people to know what's up, that there are forces at work that we can't see, you know?"

"Do you really think that? Or is this just some kind of social experiment?"

"I'm not just fucking with people, no. Why? Is this freaking you out?"

We talked there until the end of my shift, three hours later, and then we went to her place, which was right around the corner. And she read my tarot cards, and I wanted to tell her everything. Tell her how sweet she was. Tell her about me. But I knew she wasn't the same. And I gave her that good shower, just like I knew I would.

I moved my stuff in, and she understood about my mom, had all the scars to prove it. I became manager at Kinko's, and Jenny worked at a witchcraft bookstore. Gave tarot readings on the weekends and cashiered Monday, Tuesday, Wednesday. She wanted to have kids after a few years, and I wanted to tell her about me. Or for the stuff inside me to die. Just wither away.

Sometimes a while would go by, and nothing, and I would start to get hopeful. But then the sleep stuff would come. I could feel that the dreams were trying to tell me secrets. I would wake up, fully conscious, and be unable to move or scream. Be completely paralyzed, pinned down by the thoughts trying to make the new history. I didn't want it, could hardly bear it anymore.

And Jenny would tell me I said some fucked up shit in my sleep sometimes. And I wonder what she knew, in her own weird way of knowing. And I would picture that old brown and orange linoleum, and hear my mom's voice on the phone. I'd feel Doctor E's leg touching mine while we sat on that cold bench. And I knew I never wanted to saddle another woman with the burden of me again.

It's eating away at me more and more lately. The thoughts are clanging bells in my ears all the time now. I can barely hear

Jenny over the clamor anymore. And now there are new whispers. Under all that noise, suddenly, I'm hearing the pills in the medicine cabinet whistling to me, the razors murmuring in their plastic, the possibility of knotted sheets cooing. And my mother, buried under the blue sea of all that, waiting to finally hear my spill my secrets, set us both free.

TUMBLE

"It's ok to want." ***She says it so matter-of-fact.***
Her expression betrays nothing. She looks right in his eyes,
brave.

"Ok." He isn't sure what she means. As usual. He is
thrown off his center by her. Severely.

***

Because He and She got there early enough to snag it, He
and She are sitting in a round booth in a bar called The Den in a
city called New York on a planet called Headtrip.

He had called when he said he was going to and so she
jumped in the shower while he took the train over. She wanted him
to come up, but didn't ask. Instead, she met him on the stoop.

He didn't know what he was doing there exactly but he
did know that she smelled good, and she knew he looked good,
and it was warm, which was good, and they walked to The Den

feeling that good dirty sultry evening air on their skin.

So now, He and She are sitting next to each other, but not next to each other.

Before, He and She had hung out together, but not Hung Out. Together.

It's been circumstantial. This is different. There are no bonus birds being killed with this stone. No convenience. They are just straight hanging the fuck out.

He bought the first round, like he was supposed to, and she bought the second, and then he bought the third, which they are now plowing through. She's been doing Greyhounds and he's on Jack and Coke.

He asks her if she actually likes the taste of grapefruit juice. Tells her he doesn't get the appeal. That grapefruits taste how orange juice tastes right after brushing your teeth. She explains how it cuts the vodka-ness in a nice way, and offers him a sip, which he takes. He concedes that it's way better than he expected, and he's all lively behind the eyes.

She tells him about how she used to drink JD like a fish in high school, mainly because she's never liked beer. How she vomited rivers of blood-streaked Tennessee sour mash on prom night.

She is flirting with the cocktail waitress, who is really hot, and flits by occasionally. She and waitress-girl exchange compliments, act conspiratorial, tease innuendo out of each other. All during the span of three or four sips. In that way girls can pull off. They are on a first-name basis. He is impressed with the game she runs, and aware of the way she disarms. It occurs to him from a different angle, and then he throws back a large swallow, clunks the glass back on the sticky table.

She mentions how she used to cocktail herself, did that job for years, and would have to turn her head while balancing a tray of drinks with whiskey, bourbon, scotch, whatever, because the smell still got to her. He wonders if his Jack Daniels breath would gross her out. Feels awkward, insecure. Wonders if she was trying to tell him something.

She wasn't. She wasn't thinking that at all. She likes his breath.

He is saying a lot, because she is asking a lot of questions.

She likes to hear him run his mouth. She's enjoying this, and because of that, he's enjoying talking about himself more than usual. They are both buzzed and there is music blasting. The DJ keeps alternating - in an ironic-Alphabet City-hipster-bar way - between early gangster rap, new wave, and Latin.

She is lubed up from the vodka and absentmindedly breaks into "Colors" when Ice-T comes on. He is fascinated but also stymied, as he was right in the middle of his pontification on religion. He'd been giving her the whole god-is-a-product-of-a-society-looking-for-answers-to-the-unanswerable speech when the bass line kicked in. He catches her singing along with "Little 15" on a trip to the bathroom, but can't be sure if he's heard this song before.

Not just that, but when the Latin stuff comes on? She jumps up and starts salsa-ing right there at the table. But not too big. Not like she's showing off. More like she doesn't give a fuck and has to move. And the bar is crowded enough now to where it really isn't an exhibitionistic maneuver at all. She can lose herself like that.

The way she dances makes him feel like a little kid gripping a butter knife, tempted by an electric socket. It's beautiful. He wants to vibrate with it, let it run all through him. Still, though, she scares the shit out of him.

***

There's a Latin song on. For now she's just sitting in the booth. Kind of wiggle-shimmying her shoulders a bit. She's still staring at him. She sucks her drink through a straw, by leaning forward to the table, without using her hands. She never takes her eyes off him.

"So?" she stretches the o out on the end like a cat after a nap.

He has no idea where she is going with this.

"So...what?" He impersonates her inflection.

"So nothing, whatever, it's ok to want. That's all I'm saying." She looks at his hands.

"Ok."

"You know that, right?" She imagines those hands on her skin.

"Yes."

"So, then, tell me what you want."

"What do you mean, in general?" He wonders what would happen if he pressed his leg against hers under the table. Imagines her quickly slipping her thigh to rest on top of his.

"Sure."

"Ok." He scratches his jaw. "Fuck. I dunno. Success? Gratification? Peace? Satisfaction?"

"Too vague."

"Sorry."

She wants to say what she means but she's too afraid and she can't figure out how exactly. And she isn't even sure what she means. Or what she wants. Not exactly. She is saying to him what she'd wanted him to say to her. Every time she rolls it around in her mind it looks like something else. It's like reading tea leaves.

She wants the easy job.

She's angling. "Let me just ask you something."

"What?" He is watching her skin in the dim light.

"Can I ask you something?"

"You just did."

"Well, can I ask you something else?"

"Shoot."

"Don't you feel..." She senses that she's in danger of slipping down a rabbit hole, stops mid-question. Catches herself at the brink. She fancies herself the queen of mixed signals. A reluctant master at both giving and receiving. She is making a concerted effort to not fuck this up. She wants to maintain. She will inevitably have to face him again. She is riddled with heart-shaped bullet holes.

She wants the easy job.

She wonders if she's already a goner, tumbling, tossing tattered scraps of dignity and power in her wake.

He can't help himself. Puts her half-phrase back on the table:

"Don't I feel what?"

"Don't you feel like there's something between us?"

"Something like what?" He feels something, alright. He feels the rug being pulled from under him. He can't tell what the right answer is. He is being tested. He isn't wanting to fail, not at all. He does not know how to get around or over someone like her. He is as still as he can muster, hoping to lessen the possibility of a misstep. He likes to play at invisibility. He is a fugitive, crouching behind a big wall.

She is rounding the corner, a beat cop with a flashlight. "Something. Some Thing! A thing. Between us."

"A thing?"

"Yes!"

He likes her earnestness, prods it like a sea anemone. "What kind of thing?"

"You don't feel like there's a connection between us?"

He considers this, offers just enough, and it's tricky. "I feel like, I'm...I'm here, aren't I?"

She concedes. "Yes you are. You're here."

"With you."

"With me." She feels like she's won, a little bit. She's up one. "So then, you are acknowledging that there is an attraction between us?"

"Are you saying you're attracted to me?" He asks it like she's busted.

"No. I said...no, I asked...if you were willing to acknowledge that there is something going on here. Between us."

"But are you?" He can't help himself.

"Am I what?"

"Attracted to me?" He waits.

She counters. "Are you attracted to me?"

"I asked you first!"

She holds position. "Technically, I asked you first."

He tosses it right back. "But are you attracted to me?"

She considers her next move very carefully. "Well. What if I were?"

Match point. They're neck and neck again.

He proceeds with equal trepidation. "I'm just...where I'm at is..."

She rolls her eyes.

He continues. "I really...you know how it is...don't make this all messy and complicated...don't get all, you know..."

"Fuck that." She looks around for the cocktail waitress, muttering. "You're a fucking pussy."

"What?" He waits for her to respond. Nothing. "Are you kidding me?"

She won't let him off the hook. "You're trying to trick me. You're trying to get me to take all the responsibility for this, this, this thing that's between us and I'm not gonna fucking do it. You are complicit. Speaking of, why are you here, since you brought that up? Why did you come out?"

"I dunno." He really wants to give her the truth. "I guess because I like you and I like talking with you and I felt like I should."

"Should? Fuck a should! Why should you? I ain't obligating you to do shit. This was your idea. You brought it up, you called! Don't put that on me."

"You said we should hang out," He reminds her.

"Because you said you needed to tell me something," She reminds him.

He cocks his head to the side. And what squirms out of his mouth is, "Oh! So, you were just doing me a favor? Some charity counseling session? I thought we were friends. I don't need any more drama."

"Well, I thought we were drama. I don't need any more friends."

"Oh, really?"

"Yup."

"It's like that?"

"Uh huh." They look away. She plays with her straw and he fucks with his cellphone.

"Waiting for a call?" She laughs.

"Nope."

Hotty cocktail girl comes back, smoothes her hair with one hand, then places it on her hip. "Hey you two, 'nother round?"

He answers quickly. "Put it on my tab."

The waitress winks and ambles off. Neither speak until well after round four arrives. Three sips of fresh Greyhound, and she turns and looks at him. Damn it. He is so fucking hot. So beautiful, it aches somewhere specific inside her ribs. Damn him. This is not going according to plan at all. The plan is to not feel. He is fucking up her scheme.

She smiles, with no agenda, and she asks, "You want more of this shit? I can't believe you got another round. I thought we would be out of here."

"You wanna bail?"

"Nope. Do you?"

"I bought another round, didn't I?

"Yup."

What he wants is sturdy ground. His bearings. He wants to know how she really feels. He wants her to give him a straight answer. He imagines her simultaneously coming and crying in spite of himself. It just pops in his head. He sees her face on the pillow beneath him, trusting and strong, sees her two fistfuls of gripped sheets. He wants to touch that, but can't see the path. He wants to bury his breathing in her warm hair, to hijack her tongue, to crush against her, new and familiar all at once. She reminds him of someone he never met and he is worried this might mean trouble.

She wants to tell him everything. That she has been all jacked up lately. Can't think straight, completely distracted. That her head is a symphony of second guesses. She imagines what the nape of his neck would feel like against her palm. She wants to press her ear against his ribcage. She wants his lips, the crush and tumble of abandon, she wants tangled limbs. She wants to feel his torso sidelong her.

She's gonna implode if she doesn't handle this now-or-never-feeling shit. She is hamstrung.

He is hogtied. He can't see the forest for the trees in all this wilderness.

She bursts. "Well, fuck! Somebody say something!"

"You just did."

"My heart is beating outside my chest. I can't tell if I'm excited or angry."

"Can you see me?"

"I'm looking right at you, dude."

He stays with his line of questioning. "Can you see me, though?"

"Can you tell me the truth? I can only see what you show me."

"You can only see what your filter lets in and your mind projects."

"Well. Thanks, Yoda."

"How do we do this? Seriously, woman, how do we fucking do this? Something got fucked up along the way."

"Multiple things got fucked up along the way. Inside both of us. Long before we ever even met each other."

"True that." He grumble-laughs.

"Well something's gotta give...right? One of us has to give."

"The standoff. The showdown." He has his arms unfolded. One along the back of the booth, and one on the table. "Well. Do we want to kiss?"

"Do you wanna kiss me?" She levels him.

"Do you wanna kiss me?" There are three battles underway. One battle inside her, one battle inside him, and one between the two of them. He's up on his feet, decision made. "Don't say anything, I'm closing the tab."

"Get mine too, then. Please. Thanks. Ok." She slumps back against the booth.

He goes to the bar and comes back with both credit cards, two receipts for each of them, and one pen. They sign their little slips and walk out into the nighttime. It is hollow and wide after the bar air.

She wants to touch him, but past-tense has burned her frozen. He wants to put his hand on the small of her back, but remembers what an empty hand feels like, too. There are other people all around them.

They walk in tandem back towards her apartment building, her stoop. The clusterfuck thins out after a block or three. They are wordless. They had left, gone outside for a reason, but it wasn't to get to the end of this so abruptly.

She feels like she was going to tell him something but forgot what it was, like every word she pulls off the shelves of her brain is ill-equipped to label what she means.

He feels like he wants her mouth against his, but cannot tell the price.

When they get to her stoop, she stands there, fiddling her keys back and forth, looking up at him, twisting inside, then looking back down at her compelled hands. He is pulling backwards, so subtly she can feel it more than see it, towards the train station. She wants him to still her fingers and wriggling keys, to enclose all that in the large cup of his hands.

He wants her to lean into him.

There is a moment just then, when everything floats: timeless, still, stationary, and pure. Right.

And then it falls away.

He hugs her clunkily, like they don't fit at all.

She lets go of the hug a millisecond after he does, and is annoyed at herself for that show of weakness.

He starts out walking backwards. He turns towards the street, then turns back to her, a mouthful of nonchalance.

"Ok, then"

"Ok."

"See you later." He knew he would. See her. Later. But not really.

She knew it too. "Yup. See you. Get home safe."

"You too."

"I'm home. I'm not going anywhere."

"Oh yeah. Well, you know what I mean."

"Sweet dreams."

"Sweet..."

But they are both gone, already toppled. Already tumbling. Already down. Down. Down.

THERAPY

When the glass goes into my skin, I like it near
the soft part of my wrist, below my thumb. The little hollow that
shows up next to the chickeny tendon when you flex your hand
in. It feels like a burning but also kind of like a dirty itch. When I
do it, it's super hot and then I can feel the cold and wet real fast
right after.

When I am doing it is the only time I can get my head to
not think about anything else. It's like meditating or getting high
or playing the choking game or like when I used to play piano at
grandma's house when I was little and she got me lessons and
she said I was really good.

Or like when me and Jaime used to take cars. That rush
where everything floods and your mind can rest for a second.

Jaime and I finally got caught, I spit in the cop's face.
The judge gave Jaime fifteen months; me, six months followed
by two years probation, because I had prior offenses. I'm sixteen

or it could have been way worse even. One was for prostitution when I was fourteen, and one last year for possession of meth with intent to sell. Since I'm locked up, I have to take my thrills where I can get them.

I like to do it most during Family Planning class. Family Planning class is where Sister Juliet comes to the camp to talk to us about not fucking. About how abstinence is the only choice. How we are all going to get AIDS. How important condoms are. Ain't none of use getting dick in here though, so what the fuck? How she understands exactly how we feel, because she grew up on the same streets. I think she's full of shit.

She brings these really real-looking newborn baby dolls for us to baby-sit. It's to teach us how hard it would be to have a kid, but mostly all us girls fight over the dolls. I figure me and Taneka should get priority when it comes to holding them, since we are the only two actual pregnant girls in the Family Planning class. Taneka is four months and I am five months.

Since mine is gonna be born while I am still inside, and I have no one for them to give the baby to, they're gonna put her in foster care until I get out.

My mom's in Vegas stripping and she also can't stop using heroin. At least that's what my p.o. tells me. She found her. My p.o. knows that Jaime is in jail too, and his parents don't want shit to do with this baby. I don't give a fuck about that, I don't want his bitchass parents touching my baby anyway.

I don't get scared, but I do lie awake on my cot sometimes, I dunno if I am gonna get her out of foster care that easy once I'm on the outs. For example, it's for sure that the doctors know the gender, but they won't tell me officially. They say they don't want me to get attached.

But I know she's a she though.

I feel her whispering inside me for sure, and she is a girl.

I hear bad stories from other girls in the camp. Gonzales said that her cousin had a baby inside that they placed with some family, and she still hasn't found it. The system keeps confusing her and tricking her.

When I cut myself, I do it under the metal table. The class is held right in the same big cement block building where we eat sleep shit shower read pray fight masturbate cry have drama and also have class. We sit at this thing that is like a picnic table you'd see in the park, only it's metal instead of wood. So we are all sitting pretty close together, and close to Sister Juliet.

I pull the piece of glass out of my pocket. I found it in a corner of the shower stall the first week I was here. I was so happy but I knew I had to grab it and stash it before staff saw what I was doing. I got it and I got it from right under their nose and I rub it now like a rosary.

I hold both my hands under the table and I finger that soft place on my wrist. Slowly and with tenderness. And then I point the sharpest part of the glass into the flesh. I feel it press in and the skin gives until it splits open and then it's too easy. I can feel everything; I can do it good, even though I can't see what I am doing.

It's like those girls who can put their lipstick on perfectly without a mirror. I pull it up a little, like opening a zipper, like a boat creating a wake, and I can feel dripping, and the itching tingle up through my fingers.

I put my dirty thumb up against the cut after shoving the glass back in my pocket. I count slowly to two hundred inside my head and press hard. If I get caught with blood on my khakis, I get sent to psych again, and they will put me on pills. I know they aren't good for my baby.

Medina, who is one of the girls in here who is a cholo, not a chola but a cholo, told me they are testing new drugs on us. We're fucking lab rats or some shit. Drugs that have never been used before. They are gonna do some shit that will make my baby be born deformed or mentally fucked up or something.

Medina wears her hair short and combed back, but puffy on top, and she has a little moustache. On the outs I know just how she must've been treated. Like a freak by the girls, and the boys probably beat the shit out of her. But she probably took it, and so they let her be a runner or some low level shit like that.

Inside it's a whole different story. She is the hottest property. Her and Campos, who looks like Medina, only taller, and skinnier, with big green eyes. The girls inside get pretty good at using their imagination. They need men to be up on, and Medina and Campos are happy to be next best. As much as they can get away with anyway. Staff always breathing down everyone's neck.

I let Medina hold me sometimes when she climbs in my bed in the middle of the night. I think about Jaime, and what if he found out. And then I wonder if he isn't doing the same thing with some little boy he can pretend is a girl in the dark. It makes me feel real fucked up inside.

I pick my scabs sometimes when there's no way to get the glass out of my pocket and not get caught. I have to be careful in bed; the sheets are white white white. I press and count to two hundred.

At Jaime's birthday party two years back, I surprised him. He thought I couldn't come. But I planned it all out. I had his boy Chuy give me a ride over. When I got to the party, Jaime was in the bathroom. Luis told me that, right when I walked in. All them held their cans of beer to their chests, eyes widening, so obvious.

This was why I surprised him: I thought he might be creeping. So I brought this piece of steel pipe with me just in case. Jaime had given the pipe to me a while back, for when I had to walk home alone sometimes. I couldn't feel anything else, just that good concentrating feeling where there is only one thing on my mind. I started hitting the door to the bathroom, near and on the handle. Luis started tripping, because this was his mom's place. But everyone could pretty much tell that coming near me was not a good idea.

The door came down so easy; I was wondering where was the candy. And Jaime was in there with his pants around his thighs and some bitch on her knees sucking him off.

Jaime knew who I was before we even got involved. He knew what to expect in a situation like this.

I made sure not to even look at the bitch's face, because I didn't want any chance of feeling sorry for her to come over me. I wanted to swing straight at her head, see it bust like a melon, but there was a grip of people watching, and I knew I could kill her with one hit, that's how pissed I was. So instead I aimed lower and started in on her left hip. She fell over screaming. I landed two more and then just once to the chest, just to knock the breath out of her, just to shut the bitch up.

I left, and I left Jaime with no doubt about where I stood after that. He never thought to disrespect me again. Next time could be him. I heard later that she never went to a doctor or the cops, too scared to press charges, and that she couldn't walk right anymore.

Sister Juliet asks me if I love my man. If I know what commitment is. If I plan to make the best of a bad situation.

I show her a picture of me and Jaime that we got taken at the fair, all old-fashioned wild west. She says I look prettier inside here, with no hairspray in my hair, just a ponytail, and no liner on my eyes and lips. When she says that, it makes me almost want to tell her about that bitch from the birthday party for some reason. Maybe just to see her mouth hang open like a garage, see how much she really is "just like us", see what streets she's really from.

But I don't say anything, instead, I reach inside my pocket, finger the little piece of glass. Press hard against it. Feel my baby girl press hard against me. From inside.

THE WAY BACK

Tania could smell hot dogs spiraled in bacon sizzling on the 1:37 a.m. Hollywood corner. She could hear the cacophony of drunk dudes. Laughing on cell phones, trying to kick it to random trashy girls - who, Tania prayed, had to know better - one last time before peace-ing out, yelling for their boys so they could rally the troops and bounce.

She could hear them, but she was concentrating. Concentrating on the rhythmic click-click of the high-heel tips on her new you-know-you-want-some-of-this sandals. Listening to the way the concrete received her steps.

The shoes weren't brand spanking new, just virgins. Cherry now popped. On their maiden voyage. She'd bought them twenty-two days ago. Fell in love from outside the boutique on Melrose. Spent far too much money and lived on peanut butter and carrots for the next week, until her paycheck arrived like it was water and the week was forty days and she was Jesus and her shitty studio apartment was the desert.

She'd had no recent occasion to wear such fanciness, such high-heeled-ness, until this evening. And even tonight, they were far from the most sensible choice, being that she lived too close to the bar to justify driving, yet far enough away to make the walk uncomfortable, tiny little blisters already rubbing into raw pink spots under the crisscross of black leather.

On the walk to the bar, the stinging had seemed worth it, a small price to pay for so much hotness. Now, only one block in, the walk back seemed Job-worthy. She felt like a fucking fool-ass dipshit sucker.

Click click click click. She weaved dice-ily through the wasted fools. Her teeny leopard-print purse swung from the crease of an elbow, arms folded across her boobs, shoulders chilly in a stringy tank top. She concentrated on the click. A second riff started in, slapping over her solo. Male feet, comfortable and easy in their Adidas. Thud thud thud thud. Faster and off-tempo with her click.

She didn't turn around. She didn't have to. She knew who it was. She was neither pleased nor dismayed to hear Ryan's approach. She hadn't started clicking down the street to elicit any response from him. She had left because she was done. Looked like Ryan wasn't.

"Tania!" He added his tenor to the hollering-drunk-dude-chorus. "Tania, wait up!" Because she wasn't trying to run away, he reached her quickly, and swooped around to stand directly in her path. "Tania. Hey. What the fuck? Where are you going?"

"Home." Tania kept clicking and he thud-thudded backwards, staying face-to-face, avoiding her potential sidestepping of him.

"What happened?"

"You were there. You know what happened."

Ryan placed his hands on her shoulders. "Stop. Stop walking. Please. Stop. I'm gonna break my neck. I'm buzzed."

Tania stood still. Shifted her weight to her right hip. Then her left. Ryan stared like he didn't speak the language. Tania tightened her arms around herself. "Ok. I stopped."

"Thank you. Jeez." His hands were still on her shoulders. "Why did you bail?"

"How can you really not know the answer to that question?" She looked down, from his stripey t-shirt to his baggy pants to his black sneakers. Then up at his pure face. His beautiful sweet face. "Basically. Basically. Ryan. I've had enough of this shit. This is some crazy bullshit. I've wasted way too much time on this little tragedy of errors. I feel like a Smiths song."

"Who're the Smiths?"

"See? See? That's exactly what I'm talking about. I can't hang. I can not. The deal is: I have given seven months of my quickly-evaporating lifespan to nonsense. Seven months! And we haven't even kissed or anything. I shouldn't even be giving you the time of day, let alone over half a year. I shouldn't. And you. You should be working twice as hard to earn your keep. You should be bending over backwards. You should be proving yourself. I should be done with this. This is my fault. I mean, what the fuck is wrong with me? But really? What. The fuck. Is wrong. With you? Are you crazy?" She was playing all cocky.

"For not wanting us to have a one night stand? That makes me crazy? That makes me walk-out-on-able?"

"Y'know...do you know what? There's these scientists that have been studying teenagers' brains. Like the actual brains. Trying to figure out why they do such stupid-ass shit. And you know how the frontal lobe is where impulse control and decision making is like...arbitrated?"

"No."

"Yes it is."

"No, I mean, I didn't know that. Is that like, some normal thing that everybody knows except me? Like the Smiths?"

"Who cares? I was asking rhetorically. The point is that that is, in fact, a big part of what the frontal lobe does. Help handle emotions and responses to them. So that we don't just slit our wrists every time we're sad. Or punch someone every time we're mad."

"Or walk out of a bar without even saying goodbye to the person you're there with?"

"Do I seem emotional right now? Driven by uncontrollable feelings?" Ryan considered answering Tania's wild-eyed query, then thought better of it. It was yet another rhetorical question in any case.

43

She continued. "And you know what these scientists discovered? The part of the frontal lobe that regulates the emotions? Well, it doesn't fully develop until way way way later than was initially thought. In females, the shit doesn't firm up until around twenty-four. Ask me when guys' shit is all formed. Ask me!"

"When?"

"When they are twenty-eight. That means that you, Ryan Elias Zigler, don't know shit. Your opinions, decisions, they can't hurt me, because they are the musings of an undeveloped brain. You are like, mentally challenged. Twenty-motherfucking-eight. So you...you're like, not even a fully formed human. You won't be a man for six more years. At least. And that is just an average. You could be a late blooming frontal lobe-er for all I know."

"I'm twenty-five. I'll be twenty-six in like two weeks."

"Closer to three weeks. Nineteen days."

"Eighteen days now, it's two a.m. or something."

"That's still closer to three weeks than two!'

"But still, I mean, even twenty-five is not six years from twenty-eight, Tania. Not even."

"What-the-fuck-ever! I don't give a shit. It's too late at night for mathematical quibbling. The point...the point...the point of this is you're too young for me. You don't even have a completed brain yet. I'm thirty-four." This was a lie. Tania was thirty-seven.

Ryan was lying too. Tania had peeked at his driver's license once. They'd stopped for gas on their way back from an art-snob party in Malibu two months back. Ryan (who had - with his own curious and pathetic brand of magnanimity - just contributed six bucks to the fuel fund,) ran in to use the AM/PM bathroom.

His wallet, which he had tossed on the passenger seat, sat there like a pack of cigarettes, a chocolate bar, a line of blow, a love letter to someone else.

Ryan was twenty-one. Tania composed her face into something unsurprised by the time Ryan bounded back out to the car like a puppy.

"You know what? Fuck those scientists. This is lame."

"It's moot. It's moot Ryan. It's the mootest point in all of mootness. Why bother telling me you're such a man? Fine. You're

44

a big ol' manly man. You are all man all the time. You're all grown up. Yay for you. Fuck data. Fuck hard scientific fact. The fact is, the only really important fact is, you don't want me."

"Don't want you?"

"Don't want me. Yup. That's what I said. You're taking up space in my life."

"Taking up space in your life?"

"God, Ryan, what are you, my fucking voice mirror echo thing whatever? Can't you say something else? Know what? On second thought, don't say anything. Go away. Stop taking up space. Gimme my space back." Tania was terrified. She didn't want that space back. She just wanted Ryan to fill it out better. "I need that space for a man. A real man."

Ryan laughed. This wasn't helping. "Come on Tania. You're like, my best friend."

"No, I'm like, you're stand-in girlfriend. And you're like, my stand-in boyfriend. But I am not hot enough or whatever for you. You don't want me. I am done."

"T-yizz, don't do this."

Tania kept on clicking towards home. She was pretty much there. "I'm not doing anything. I'm done doing." Neither spoke for the final stretch. She turned towards her building.

Ryan held back, stayed on the sidewalk. "Tania! Tania. I'll call you tomorrow."

Tania spoke without looking back. "Ok."

***

Tania had promised herself, tonight would be it. One more time out with Ryan, and that was it. She would lay her cards on the table. Put it out there. No more guessing. And whatever Ryan said, that would be that. She would cut the cord tonight. She'd been strung out on this long enough. And that's what she did. Kind of.

Ryan had called around nine p.m. as usual. "Whassup, T-T-T-Tanyizzle?"

"Hey Ry Ry." Tania unfurled herself, her back on the floor, and made the wiggle of delight leave her voice.

"Are you smoking a cigarette?"

"Ryan. I haven't smoked in three months or something." She threw the smoldering butt in the nearly-gone glass of wine, and reminded herself to exhale more quietly on the phone.

"Well, not cigarettes, anyway..." He laughed.

"Uh-huh."

"Y'know Tania, you don't have to lie to me, I don't care if you smoke cigarettes. I mean, I don't want you to, obviously, 'cause it's bad for you, y'know, but I'm not judging you."

"Phew. Thanks, Ry. That's a lot of weight off my shoulders."

"Have you been drinking?"

Tania took the glass into the bathroom and dumped the dirty pinkish filter, which had soaked up the last remnants of cheap red wine, into the toilet. Then she peed. "Nope. I don't just sit around drinking and smoking myself into oblivion while I pine away, waiting to hear from you."

"Did you just flush the toilet? Were you pooping while you were on the phone with me? Clas-sic!" Ryan laughed.

"No, dude, sorry to destroy your fantasy, I wouldn't even pee on the phone with you, let alone take a dump."

"Alright, got it, so...what are we getting into tonight?"

This was it. This was the crux of why shit had to change, like five minutes ago. Ryan was getting comfortable. Entitled. Assuming that she was free. Assuming that they would be doing shit together every night. It was all the stifled feelings and suppressed impulses and resentment that came with being in a real-live relationship. And none of the sex. The fact that Ryan was assuming correctly had little-to-nothing to do with it, in Tania's mind.

Ryan came to her place. They smoked a joint he had brought, then walked down to Hollywood Boulevard. Nearly every bar between Wilcox and Vine had a theme. It was like the Disney people had added a new annex to the Happiest Place On Earth: Hornydrunkposerland. The gimmick at Star Shoes was very loosely executed. A few glass cases here and there with some vintage pumps in them. Whatever. Cheesy, but proximate.

A Tribe Called Quest floated off the turntables and billowed through the room. People said, "Ohhhhh!" and then,

"Bo knows this (what) and Bo knows that (what)…" Most people were bouncing to the beat and lots of them were singing along, every word. Tania was contemplating the fact that she and Ryan made a demographic sandwich out of this joint. They were the two skinniest outer reaches of the bell curve. Everyone else here fell between their ages. She snorted at this and turned around to tell Ryan her little revelation. He'd been walking through the crush of people right behind her, but now he was gone. Lost in a sea of likewise-striped t-shirts and floppy haircuts.

Before she could start looking in earnest, she felt something cold against her neck and spun around. There he was, with a goofy grin on his face and two fistfuls of Long Island Iced Tea. One which had spilled a bit after Tania jerked her head from it. He held it out to her, an offering. The other, he was sucking down like chocolate milk.

Tania tried to look just a bit tired of his antics. He really was adorable. Obviously. Why else would she still be in this mess?

"Aww, Ry Ry, you know who you look like?"

"Chingy? *Holiday Innnnn!*"

"Not really so much. Remember those old Hershey's Syrup commercials?"

"Um, which ones?"

Tania took her Long Island to her mouth and imitated him sucking from the straw. He looked blank. She slurped up some more. Made her eyebrows go up and down, made her eyebrows say, *get it? Get it? Get it?* Ryan was nonplussed. "Come on, Ryan. Messy Marvin? Hello?"

"I dunno Messy Marvin."

"Yes you do. Oh god. No you don't. You really don't. It's hard for me to remember that people born in the eighties are let into clubs. It's hard for me to wrap my head around it. But you know Messy Marvin."

"I don't. I'm sorry, seriously, he sounds like a heck of a guy."

"But Ry, you do, seriously. I feel so much better. You know what else Messy Marvin was in? I mean not literally the character of Messy Marvin, but the actor who played him, Peter Something-or-other. A Christmas Story. Everybody knows A Christmas Story." Tania breathed a genuine sigh of relief.

"The one with the Ghost of Christmas Past in it? And

Stooge?"

"No. No. The one with the leg lamp. And the little kid licking the frozen pole and his tongue sticking to it. And fyi, it's Scrooge. Not Stooge. And that is called A Christmas Carol, not A Christmas Story."

Ryan nodded. "Yeah, yeah. I never saw that flick, but I know who The Three Stooges are. That's a punk band that that scrawny guy used to be in, right?"

"Right, Ry. Iggy Pop. Except they're called The Stooges. The Three Stooges are something else."

"What?"

"Never mind. Thanks for the drink, by the way. It's nice to be bought a drink, makes me feel like a lady."

"Cheers!" he clunked his glass against hers, even though they'd both been working on them already.

"How'd you get them so fast? The bar is packed. You were right behind me, and then you were gone, and then you were back like, a second later."

"Oh dude, check this out, T-yizz! My boy Jimmy got a job barbacking here! Nice! He totally hooked it up, yo! Free drinks, all night, unless he gets fired. That's why I wanted to come here."

"Rad."

"You wanna come meet Jimmy? Come over, he's hella cool. He has a tattoo of a koi that goes almost all the way around his neck."

"Let's totally do that a little later, ok? I wanna sit down."

Tania and Ryan walked to the only empty-ish area in the bar, a banquette-y thing in the giant storefront window.

Tania stared at Ryan. It was most definitely go time. She had to say or do something. Anything. Ryan grinned and punched her in the arm, asked, "Whassup, kiddo?"

Tania almost choked on her Long Island. "Kiddo? Um, no, you can't call me kiddo."

Ryan punched her again. "Why not, kiddo?"

"Because I am not a kiddo. I am a woman. And you, of all people, have no place to call me kiddo." And then she just blurted it out, at this most unromantic, weirdest moment. "Fucking what Ryan, what? Fucking you want me so bad you can hardly stand it. It's on dude. It's now or never. Get on it. Grab me. Take me. Let's do this. Fucking fuck. C'mon. Fuck!" It dawned on Tania that she was still making lots of words with her mouth, when she figured she should have stopped talking by now, because Ryan should have taken some action. Said something. "Fuck."

Ryan actually was looking at her like she was a pathetic abandoned puppy. "Oh man, Tania, I think you got the wrong idea."

"Fuck that. You're in love with me."

"Oh geez Tania. I just don't feel that way about you."

"You're in love with me!" Suddenly, Tania could hear herself. Like she was outside of herself, looking at the scene like a bad movie. She was cringing for the stupid delusional spinster lady, who was her. It was unbearable.

And so she had to just walk out. It was the only thing left to do. She had to get away from who she had become. And she would. If she could. She had to try. She had to find her way back to herself, if there was anything left to her. If she could, she most definitely would.

BACKING OUT

It does something to your perspective on a
person when you see the animal come out of them. We
all got animal, you know? Some people's animal lives close to the
surface, snarling and panting and chomping at the bit, just under the
skin. Other people's animal is tiny, mousy most of the time, sitting in
the very middle of them.

Sometimes, you'll see the animal break loose when a
someone is really angry, just stuck in traffic, say. Something snaps.
Maybe you're there when someone finds out that their grandchild
was killed in a freak skiing accident. The thing about that animal is,
once it's out, once you've seen that rawness in a person, you can't
go backwards. You always have that memory.

That's what happened at the end of me and Darlene. You
know? When she finally got that I was resolute, realized that there
was no way I was gonna not-break-up with her, that there was no
saving us as an Us? She just really lost it. Lost It, because she
figured there was nothing else to lose. In that animal-raw way. I

was embarrassed for her. It made it easier.

Part of the time, she was curled up, way smaller than I would have guessed she could make herself, like a roly-poly, a pill bug. Right? And for a while she was crying and shaking and just, repeating herself a lot. Like, a lot. She was inconsolable, quivering and whimpering. "Please don't...why? Ah, fuck. Please no. Oh...why? There's something wrong with me. Why am I like this? Why does this happen to me?"

"Darlene. What can I say to that?" This was way bigger than me, like it always ends up being, at the bitter end. I wanted to reach the end of this. I rubbed her back in what I hoped was a comforting way. Felt her stiffen beneath my hand like melodrama.

"Please, Angel. Seriously. If you don't love me, don't touch me. I can't bear it. I really can't...fuck fuck fuck, why? Why Angel?"

And around in a circle it went like that. Until she finally exhausted herself. She passed out for an hour around seven am and I tried to wrap myself around her. I still wanted to feel her, to take in the smell of her. She mumbled, barely conscious, "Angel, don't be that guy, please. Please don't touch me. Don't give me hope."

She woke a little before eight-thirty, started crying again. Real quiet and mellow, tears coursing down her cheeks in streams of hot wet lost pride. The last little reserves of human worth. The last residue.

Her eyelids were so swollen they looked translucent, so swollen that the eyelashes looked like sewing needles in a pink pincushion. The edges looked segmented, like big puffy gummy worms. She was like a zombie, and then like a robot. Alternately methodically and carelessly, she placed her clothes back in the little pink gym bag that she used for weekend trips.

She'd drive from Iowa City to me in Chicago every weekend she was able. I never would go visit her in IC because for one, it's IC, and for two, my tags were expired. I didn't feel like spending money on them. It's like...Darlene made it too easy. Too easy to not put in the effort, you know? I feel bad for females. I honestly do.

She walked out to her car, wordless. I went with her. It

was freezing out, and really bright. Sunny. She tossed her bag in the backseat, still all eerily detached. She moved into my hug when I opened my arms to her. The last time I ever held her, I could feel her chest crumble in on itself. Feel her cave. And I felt bad about that. I didn't want to destroy her.

I watched her car disappear into the swallow of city traffic. And I knew I could never look at her the same after that. Once someone shows that starving hunger inside them, it changes everything. I didn't even want to smell her anymore after a little while. And then it was all gone.

***

The day before, I'd heard the voicemail from Darlene and I could not believe it. Except that I could. Should've expected it, really. She was sitting outside my apartment, in her car, she said. Said she couldn't wait to see me, to spend New Year's Eve with me. Said she hoped I'd had a good Christmas. Like she was trying to sound all positive and upbeat or something. I hit *end* on my cellphone and sucked on a Newport. Fuck.

I was in Iowa City. Fucking ironic. New Year's was like, four hours away. She was driving back from spending the holidays with her super intense family in Detroit. Stopped by on the way home. I felt like we had vaguely discussed that possibility, never set it in stone.

I smoked another cigarette and put the ringer on silent, not even vibrate. By the time I stubbed that one out, I had six missed calls. Fuck. I called her back.

"Hey, you." She answered before the first ring was even done.

"Darlene. Happy New Year."

"Aw, you too." I could hear that she was trying to sound not-pissed. Trying to be sweet. To give me the benefit of the doubt. "So hey, where are you, babe? I've been sitting out here in my car for like, an hour. It's super windy."

I laughed. Tried to warm up the news. "You're not gonna believe this. I'm in IC."

"What?" Her voice lowered a few octaves. She was trying.

"Jared's grandmother died. I came down here with him to

5 3

the funeral." My trump card. It was true and more horrible than anything, but it still felt good to put her in her place with it, watch her pull back. Jared's an old college buddy. He grew up two blocks from Darlene, and they never met until I introduced them. Funny how that can happen.

"Oh, no, is he ok? I'm so sorry."

"Yeah, he's ok. They knew it was coming, that whole thing. She died on Christmas."

And then, the brick of lame smashed through her windshield. "Oh my god, you're in Iowa City?" It hit her how twisted that really was. She had been driving a long time. I could hear all the resentment bubble up. All the frustration with how much more effort she put in snuck up on her. I was listening to it. "This sucks." She was starting to crumble. "What should I do, should I drive down there, or what?"

"Well, you know I didn't drive. And I did ride with Jared. And he wants to roll back to Chi-town soon. So."

"So if I drove down I'd end up having to drive you back to Chicago, and then having to drive my own ass back to IC in a few days, basically?"

"Well." She made me feel like such a loser all the time without even trying to. She did have to do all the work. And while on the one hand it made me feel powerful, like she was jumping through hoops, it also flipped like this to completely emasculate me.

Like, fuck. Why didn't I just get my tags? Why was I still working on my music? Shitty idm beats I couldn't even stand listening to anymore. Still grinding away dayjob-style at Elemental Records. At thirty-four. It made me want to puke.

I told her to wait there. That I would get Jared to leave soon. Still, she spent New Year's freezing, parked outside my apt. I got there around two am and we went inside. We had good sex, which didn't change anything.

***

I'd been feeling like a real loser. Darlene would send me her beats and I would seethe with jealousy. Didn't even want to listen. She was inspired, and the shit sounded good. I could picture her chain-smoking, in headphones, clicking her tongue piercing absentmindedly. Nodding. Building shit.

Darlene was blowing up. I comforted myself with the thought that she was only doing well because she was a novelty item. She was a she. Fuck, right? Her buzz was getting loud.

"Hey Angel Babe, did you get the file I put up on the ftp server?"

"Aw, I forgot to go check." I lied. The track had been sick, dnb stuff. She was bold. It was ill.

"What about the mp3 I emailed you?" I could hear her breath coming shallow, like it did when she was on a roll, inspired, working hard.

"Haven't listened yet."

"Are you busy right now?" She wasn't being pushy; she just cared what I thought. She liked that we shared this.

"No, I guess not."

"Ok, go listen and call me when you're done. I have to know what you think. None of my tracks feel real until I share them with you." She meant this, but still, it made me feel bitter. What bullshit! She had a record label in Copenhagen about to put out her first EP! Who gives a fuck what I think?

"Ok, Darlene. I will go listen and call you back."

Because I already had listened, I just stared at the computer, watching that little clock change, and smoked. The thing about it was, Darlene really wasn't rubbing my nose in it or anything like that. She still treated me like I was above her. Like I was the expert. She still admired me, my work. This girl, who I never thought would have given me the time of day, was now sprung. It was bordering on unbearable.

After almost four minutes, I called her back, told her the track was dope. Which it was.

***

Darlene deejayed, which is how I first met her. She had started that before making her own tracks, even. Think about it. Who wouldn't want to book a super hot chick dj? She was innovative, and strong in her own right. That was the truth. She wasn't one of those floozy girls or candy raver types, either. There was nothing waiflike about her at all. She was tall, with a big mass of curly dark wiry hair, and broad shoulders. Her spinning was aggressive, not cutesy.

I had booked her for an event in a Wicker Park club. I used to promote a few regular nights. I only did it because I wasn't making enough money from my own music. They were never huge ragers. I didn't want them to be too good. I didn't want to be more known as a promoter than I was as a beatmaker.

I needed some more female vibe energy for a show, and had seen Darlene do a quickie ten-minute set around four am in an after-hours club a few blocks from my apartment. That night, I had been candy flipping, and went home to sleep. When that didn't work out so well, big surprise, I left again and ended up seeing her spin.

It took me just a few phone calls to get to her and book her for the show. We were instantly tight and I wanted to kiss her from the jump, but she was out of my league. I worked on her for months. Booking her for gigs, offering to let her stay with me at my pad when she would come to town. She'd always say that I paid her well enough; she could totally afford a hotel room.

One time, she asked me to come with her instead.

"So Angel, what you getting into now?

"Just gonna go home. Smoke a fatty." Like clockwork, I gave her the now-perfunctory offer. "Come stay with me, it's free."

"Aw Angel."

I tried a new angle. "All the djs who come through do."

"But I'm not 'all the djs who come through'"

"What do you mean by that?"

"Angel...well, I'm a chick, for one."

"DJ Dawn Day stays with me."

"Yeah but Dawn does two by four with her boyfriend, remember? So he stays there too."

I was in farther than I'd ever gotten before. "Are you saying you wouldn't feel safe staying with me? Without another dude there to protect you? You look like you can hold your own. Like you can scrap."

"Of course. Please." She served it up straight: "Look, I'm

not attracted to you. That's all. That's a caveat I want to give you. If that's cool, if you're not trying to kick it to me, then for sure, grab that fatty and let's chill. But there's one more thing."

"What's that?"

"I don't mind paying for the hotel. Let's go there."

And we did. And I didn't even offer to split the hotel charge with her. I figured she owed me. And after we smoked, and drank from the miniature bottles of Stoli and Absolut, which Darlene ended up paying for too, I touched her. Just touched her arm. But the way it moved through her meant she hadn't been touched in so long, hadn't let herself be touched in so long, that it made her hunger outrun her sense. Made her barter with her dignity.

I wanted to see how far she could bend over backward. At the same time, watching her contortion act made me hate her, hate her for not blowing me off. For taking it. Made me want to shake her, ultimately. Made a small jaw clench inside me, tiny ears tip inside me, made a faint growl inside me start to grow.

DOWN STAIRS

Got this call. Like, seven a.m. There was this
two weeks-ish where I was really into blow. Had this weird out-
of-body thing happen. Found myself floating outside the window
of my Brooklyn apartment peeking in at my sleeping form. I could
see the bricks on the outside of the building. Spent lots of time in
bed. Never touched it again.

"Cara Mia, did I wake you? Shaina, do you know who this
is?"

I didn't have a clue. My head was a minefield.

Laughter crackled through the line into my ear. Man
laughter.

There's that tinny awkwardness that comes from talking to
someone on the phone for the first time. When did I give Tommy
my number?

***

I'd been living on first and eighty-sixth. Subletting from this weirdo. She used the apartment as a workspace to make beaded curtains. Even showed me some snippet about her door décor from like, ten years back. In Glamour magazine. What the fuck? Whatever, crazy lady. She was hardly ever there working. Which was more than fine.

Like all harebrained schemes, the bottom fell out. Marinda showed up one day, raging, some hackneyed bullshit about me stealing her scented oils. Upshot, she and her husband were splitting up. She needed a pad. Psycho-cunt just couldn't be real and say it.

Marinda, sitting on the couch. All scrawny, pinched up and blond. Seething with envy at my nineteen-year-old-ness. Vacillating between random glares and *The Celestine Prophecy*. Folding arms and legs, wiggling a foot while I packed right then, no choice.

First I called Paul in Brooklyn. He was always saying,

"Anytime you wanna get out of freaky deeky beady town, I got all the Rolling Rock you can drink."

Then I called a car service and got them to bring out a van. My master plan was to slip the driver a twenty and hope for the best.

I'd strapped my viola to my back the moment Marinda started in on me. It wasn't leaving my touch until I was in Paul's place. I loaded my shit down stairs. Out on the sidewalk. Starting with Gorgeous, in a cat carrier. He was hissing and spitting and pissed.

Next door was swanky Gio Ristorante. It was summer. Rich people eating out front. Me, sweating. Heaving garbage bags of underwear, lotion, cereal, et cetera.

I dropped the last pillowcase full of books I guesstimated would fit in your average soccermom mobile. Mauricio, the maitre d', began cooing supportively,

"Darling what, can I help?"

Of course, he asked right when I was done with the heavy lifting. The box of cat quivering like the devil incarnate. Fuckin' man. Fuckin' maitre d'. Could he help? Kinda, yeah. Possibly, I reckoned. If he was gonna put his money where his mouth was.

"I need a job." I lugged my stuff to the van as it rolled up,

Persian driver guy's mouth agape.

"Come by here tomorrow morning around eleven, Bella. Ciao."

I started bartending that Saturday. Dubs. Ten a.m. to two a.m. four days a week.

Lunches were mellow and trippy. That's when I met Tommy Vitale. He came in on my shift and sat down, grinning over the marble bar. Fabrizio, the manager, made eyebrows at me from the kitchen door and jerked his head back. I walked to him.

"Shaina, Tommy doesn't get a bill, he comes to lunch all the time. Dinner too. In the register, there's a leather book, his tab. He pays in full at the end of the year. Got it?"

I nodded and went back to the bar. Tommy ordered a pizza and I wrote it in the little book. Kee-rist, it was already over thirty gs. I sized Tommy up. What was his deal?

He had a face that registered at sixty, and shoe-polish black hair. He was tan and kinda short. Had a seriously bangin' body. For an old guy especially.

I brought him his pizza and watched him drizzle chili-infused olive oil and balsamic vinegar over it. He pulled up a slice.

"What's your name, you?

"I'm Shaina, nice to meet you, Tommy."

His eyebrows went north.

"Your kinda famous," I explained.

"Shaina. Pretty. How old do you think I am?"

"Thirty"

He laughed.

"I like you, Shaina. I'm seventy-five. Can you believe it? Wait until you meet my wife. She is beautiful. I exercise every day, the blood has to circulate, that's the secret."

After that, I could see the seams of plastic surgery in my imagination. Tommy was cool, he didn't give a fuck.

"Eat this piece. Eat lunch with me. I insist."

Tommy did indeed come in most days, and we ate lunch together. We shot the shit in a serious way. Turned out Tommy owned most of the real estate on that block, and a fair chunk of apartments in Trump Tower.

He knew I wanted to do music, to be home, transcribing

my head's contents into clefs. Tommy believed in me, thought I was good, even though he'd never heard a note.

He told me that if I ever needed to leave, he'd buy me a ticket home to Colorado. He was always wanting to hightail me out of the city for some reason. I guess I looked burnt. He gave me his number, just in case. I gave him mine. He asked. He was pretty persuasive.

***

Tommy, laughing hard now, "Yes, Mia, it's me, yes, sleepyhead. Guess where I am."

"Um, Manhattan?"

"No, no. Napoli!"

"Wow."

"Come meet me, Shaina, I will take care of work for you. I will call Fabrizio."

"I...don't...have a passport." It was true. It was the first thing that came to mind.

Tommy was having none of it. "Get to the airport, someone will meet you there, with papers."

"Wait, what? I can't, I don't even, I need to..."

Tommy knew my crazy living situation, how I'd ended up with that job and was just at Paul's temporarily, all the wacky circumstances. He pulled my card.

"Shaina, move into a studio at Trump Tower, I will charge you five hundred rent. A steal. But I get to keep a key. Why worry about this now? Don't. We can work it out later. Come to Italy. I have friends. La Scala."

I thought about it.

I really considered it.

My mind was flooded with opposites. Me, in gorgeous black velvet, to the floor, back in NYC, making my US debut after a glorious early career in Italy. What the fuck? Or what if this was just some crazy setup? But let's say it wasn't a setup, it was a genuine opportunity, and I just failed. Just wasn't up to it. And then Tommy just like...well...it was like I owed him? What was I fighting for? Didn't bartending, didn't the service industry, make me a whore anyway? Why not at least whore myself out to get something I wanted, at least? It was an opportunity. I didn't have to be an actual whore. I could keep myself out of trouble. Shit.

I told Tommy to call me back in a half hour. And he did. And I didn't answer. Not the second or third time either.

***

I wonder seven years backward. Stumble down the back stairs, into my backyard. It feels foreign, like someone else's, with its faded Tonka trucks and impotent garden.

My husband leaves for work. The baby's bundled off to kindergarten. Emptiness climbs, reliable and cold. I ponder this newfound relenting, the atrophying of everything. I am complacent as elevator music. Muzak.

When the soil is soft enough, I dig in the Nebraska dirt. Plant tulip bulbs over crumpled compositions no viola will ever sing.

W E S L E Y

Wesley could remember the way his skin
felt up against Skyler's. The remembering felt like dying.
The remembering felt like emptiness, like little cold spots all along
his left side, like concave parts, like indentations.

Wesley was lying in bed at three in the afternoon, and
he propped himself up on his left elbow. He stared over towards
the dinged-up vanity he'd picked up at Goodwill. Scrutinized his
reflection in the greasy mirror. He still looked good. Like a ballerina
in Swan Lake resting after dress rehearsal. He was just one of
those boys...using the term loosely, as he was nearly thirty-six...
who looked like a doe. He carried himself like Audrey Hepburn in
Roman Holiday without even trying.

Two hours of crying and the eyeliner wasn't even smudged,
hardly. Nary a mascara trail. Thank god for M.A.C.

Wesley's eyes wandered to the top of the dresser. He
blinked. Skyler's walkie talkie sat there, winking at Wesley.

Skyler and Wesley used to work together at the Pink

Pucker, at the bottom of the Castro. Here's what happened: It was Folsom Street Fair two years back, and Wesley was done up in all his regalia, and that's when he's she. When he's Wynona.

And Wynona was as much Wesley as Wesley was Wynona. Wynona is who Wesley is. She was really into pink that year, which was how she ended up working at the Fink Fucker, as she and all the other worker bitches called it. Wynona took coincidences seriously, so when Mickey offered her a job there, she jumped on it.

Pink and the stewardess-in-the-fifties look. Wynona walked through the crowds of men with their penises on leashes like a preening peacock. She was decked to the nines in clear magenta platform sandals, salmon fishnets, a so-shiny-it-looked-like-a-chocolate-easter-egg-wrapped-in-foil bikini, and a little TWA-lady pillbox hat. She'd refurbished it herself in ballet-pink and added netting. The netting came to the bottom of her eyes, which blinked slow as a cow's, all metallic rose false eyelashes and dilated pupils.

It was hot hot hot and Wynona's heart was beating a steady flamenco, e and blow coursing through her veins like a cyclone. She was walking all diva and her hips sank from left to right as she strutted over asphalt. Wynona was feeling really good, which is the only time these types of things happen.

She saw Danika first. An Asian girl body-painted with the giant face of a leopard. She was pretty eye-catching, to say the least. She was completely butt-ass-naked, her tits, painted with green eyes, and there was a triangle of cat-nose at the belly button level which stretched down to the white feline mouth that spread across her pussy. All the rest of her was covered in orange and leopard spots up to where a boatneck shirt would have stopped, below the collar bone.

In Wynona's current state of distorted mental capacity, this already-noteworthy sight was even more fascinating. She couldn't contain herself.

"Wow! Nice pussycat!" Wynona's eyes followed a chain around the tiger girl's neck to the man attached to it. Six foot three, hairless, with rippling muscles, and one arm missing. Head shaved clean-bald. No shirt. Black leather pants. Big combat boots. Wynona had never seen anyone or anything more beautiful or perfect in her entire life. The e gave her confidence. The e gave her joy. The blow gave her ballsiness. The blow gave her a sense of humor. "Hey Mister, I like your Pussy."

"This is Danika," One-armed beautiful buffed man spoke in a voice like spandex stretching over a calf.

"Hi Danika." Wynona fixed her attention on the only person there she was interested in. "But who are you?"

"I'm Skyler. I painted her myself."

"I painted me myself. Quel coincedence. I'm Wynona."

Time stood still. Planets and stars flashed. Comets grinned. The earth held her breath. Danika got bored and wanted to go look for a drink somewhere. Skyler's one hand slackened, and the chain that circled Danika's neck slipped from his loosed grip like marbles. She sauntered off. Wynona reached one of her two hands out, almost grabbing a pec before she could gain control of herself. Skyler caught her wrist in his one hand and guided her palm to his chest, placed it on the taut flesh, right over his heart. Wynona could feel the sun caught there, the warmth of outside in the skin, the gold of it all. She could feel a little stubble underneath. When she exhaled, she fell forward, and Skyler's mouth caught hers.

They fell in love hard and fast and Wynona could be Wesley or Wynona and Skyler was just as in love. Wesley got Skyler a job bouncing at the Pink Pucker, where Wynona danced five days a week. They were wrapped in the eachotherness like a magic blanket, walked to work together, and then walked home together nine hours later. It was right.

Until it wasn't. Wesley started getting sick, only wanted blow, was angry a lot. Got fired from the Fink Fucker for stealing another girl's tips while she went pee. Skyler had been begging Wesley to slow down, to stop, to get a grip, to try meditation, yoga, praying, NA, anything.

But Wesley liked to feel strong and amusing and confident and his perspective was slipping. Soon Wesley was hardly ever around, it was mostly Wynona. But Wesley was all that ever really was. At least, that was what Wynona was most afraid of.

Wesley didn't want Skyler to see all the seams coming apart inside his soul. So he avoided Skyler. But then the missing would start. And sometimes he would call Skyler. And last night was one of those nights. He begged Skyler to stop by after he got off work.

But Skyler was just worried, not in love. Not anymore. Just sad, and scared for Wesley. And Wynona. And so he came by to check. And Wesley tried to crush his mouth against Skyler's. And Skyler had had to push him down on the bed as gently as possible.   Wesley had been clawing and pulling and screaming, and then just cried a lot, and finally passed out. Which was when Skyler left, forgetting his walkie talkie- which had gotten shoved aside in all the needing and desperation and sorrow- on the vanity.

And now Wesley was watching it, staring back at it, praying to it. Because it meant he would get to see Skyler, be held by him, one more time. At least once more.

MATCH

Janet Gold's heart was a peach pit as it sank to her belly and, then it turned into an atomic fireball. Ninth grade was totally sucking already. She was so mad she was shaking all the way to her fingertips. Things had been getting weirder and weirder. This was the final straw. Total. She could see Lara Soto walking with her shanghaied best friend, Danielle Nally, as the block stretched away from her. She broke into a run before she had time to think. Listened to her converse slapping the sidewalk.

"Hey Danny, could I talk to you for a sec?"

Danielle spun around, all jeans jacket and crispy blond bangs. She attempted to look bored and blasé. Janet knew her well enough to know that the way she was chomping her gum told a different story. And Janet knew what she had just seen in 7-11. Shoplifting. Alcohol. They have like, cameras in there! Was Danielle, like, possessed? So stupid and not worth it. So stupid.

"Wh'sup, Janet?"

"Um, could I please talk to you, like, alone?"

Lara laughed in a disconcerting way and her hairspray-addled Clairol-black curls wiggled unnaturally, as a single unit. She rolled her heavily kohl-smeared eyeballs.

This was appalling. It was hard to believe. Having to ask her bff since fourth grade to talk to her? Having to ask for privacy? What crazy world was she living in? Why was God punishing her? She considered punching Lara, but quickly decided against it, 'cause she was gigantic and scary.

These two girls made her feel like some weird Jewy toad.

Danielle crossed her arms strangely, over the bulge on the inside pocket of her Levi's jacket. When did she start wearing jeans jackets anyways?

"Actually, Janet, here's the thing, we're kinda in a hurry? So..."

"I saw what you did, you guys. I saw. Danny, have you gone crazy?"

Danielle tried to blow it off but she couldn't lie for shit. Her cheeks were all red in the way that only Wasps can blush. Janet noticed that she had her collar turned up like Molly Ringwald or something. Barf!

"What are you talking about, Janet?"

"Danny, seriously, please! I was right there in the 7-11. You put a wine cooler
in your inside pocket and then you guys walked out!"

"Whatever Janet. No we didn't."

"We? Oh great, so both of you stoled wine coolers? Did you get the same flavor or a variety pack?" They just stood there. "Show me inside your jacket then. Just open your jacket if you have nothing to hide."

Queen Lara spoke, in her congested gother-than-thou glottal drawl.

"C'mon, Danny. Laters, Janet. Goody goody bitch."

Janet felt angry tears welling up and spilling out of the cups of her lower lids. The indignity of uncontrollable babyness made her even angrier.

"I can't believe this."

She couldn't even breathe right.

"I feel like I don't even know you anymore, Danny. Danny! Who are you? Oh my gosh!"

They were already disappearing towards St. Christopher's. Which was Jupiter, as far as Janet was concerned. Danielle was slipping away.

***

In eighth grade, everything started normalish. Jr. High sucked, but still, she and Danielle had each other. They withstood the indignity of adolescence as best they could. They'd lie around after school, listen to The B52s and Yaz and fantasize about frenching Simon LeBon. They spent their lunch break in the library reading about hallucinogens, stimulants, and depressants in The Encyclopedia Of Drugs, which their school inexplicably kept on the shelves.

And then. Then, the Christ-ers from the youth group at St. Christopher's started having these, like, parties, where they would like, kidnap kids and bring them to do all this fun stuff with the church. Janet never got kidnapped, and she never wished she had. Had they tried, she would've told them to fuck right off. But she still felt the sting. She knew where she wasn't wanted.

Danielle, on the other hand, had gone to some parties.

Janet was beside herself about it.

"Danny," She had said, with as much portent as she could muster, "They're trying to brainwash you! I can't believe you went to the church thing ever."

"Janet. They're Catholic, not Satan Worshippers,"

"I wish they were. That would be awesome. Interesting, at least. Jeez. D'you know they're taking a big group of kids to Disneyland, and they're gonna miss a half a day of school? 'Oh, look how fun Jesus is, we'll take you to The Happiest Place on Earth, as long as you're not a Jew or otherwise unacceptable to us.' Whatever."

"I'm going on that trip."

"Oh my god, are you serious? They probably want to kill me or something. You're supposed to be my best friend. I can't believe you're going to Disneyland with them. Your mom is letting you do that?"

"Janet. Duh. Of course. It's a *church youth group*."

Janet briefly considered calling Danielle's mom and telling

her that she didn't trust these people. She knew it was hopeless though. Once, when she and Danielle were in sixth grade, after a movie, Danielle's mom was like, twenty minutes late to pick them up, as usual. Janet convinced Danielle to climb the marquee with her. Janet had found a J with a corner broken off on the ground. It had fallen from the sign. She decided that Danielle needed a D for herself. So they went up there and stoled one.

When Danielle's mom figured out from the front seat what had happened, she turned the car around in a righteous huff and demanded that they bring the letters back in and apologize.

But Janet had stood her ground, at least regarding the J.

"Mrs. Roberts," Danielle's mom was on her third husband, "Mine isn't actually stoled, 'cause it broke and fell on the ground. Lookit, it's all scratched up. The only reason I even found it is 'cause we were bored waiting for you to come get us."

Hm. Christ-ers vs. Janet the klepto Jew. Danielle's mom would never have listened to her. Great. Janet didn't stand a chance.

August before Frosh year, they were hanging out in their favorite store, The Underground. It was definitely the coolest place in their boring awful town. It was where they bought all the Duran Duran and Depeche Mode and Adam Ant pins that decorated their Jansport backpacks. There was this back room they weren't allowed into. You had to have a driver's license that said you were eighteen. Danielle had heard from Nicholas Sherman that they sold bongs back there, but you had to call them tobacco water pipes when you asked for them, or they'd kick you out. Amber McManus from French class told Janet that they sold dildos and other sex toys like that.

Danielle and Janet were sitting cross-legged on the ground, flipping through the poster displays, drooling over dreamy boys. The store was big, and wooden, and it was easy to disappear back there. Janet had found some matches that were supposed to be like miniature incense and was trying to light them. They were crumbly and weird and wouldn't strike properly.

"Danny, look at these, they are so random. They would be cool for pooping. You know how people light matches when they poop?"

"Ew, yeah, I don't get that. Then it just smells like sulphur and burning poo combined."

Janet laughed.

"I know! Total. People are so weird. I would never poop in public. What would you do if you really had to poop at school? Would you go or hold it?"

"Hold it."

"School is mondo stress-mo. High School is gonna suck. But it has to be better than Jr. High, right? Dreamy Senior boys with better taste in music and Vespas, at least."

Janet was still absentmindedly whisking the rose-scented matches across the back of their book.

Danielle kept her eyes on the posters.

"Hopefully...St. Christopher's will be better."

"Yay for them." The realization hit her hard. "No way. Danielle. You're going to St. Christopher's? Oh. My. God. What? Wait, what?"

Her hands were moving furiously now. The match she was pressing ignited. But a chunk of the head stuck in her finger. On fire.

"Ow, ohmigod, ow, Danny, I'm on fire! Owee. Oh no!"

Danielle wanted to help but didn't know what to do.

"Shhh, Janet, you're gonna get us in trouble! Smoosh it or grab it or something, are you ok? You're gonna get busted for even lighting those without buying them."

It was already out, but her skin was burnt good. There was a gray blister on the tip of her finger, with the piece of match still in it. It alternated between numbness and sore awful throbbing for almost a week.

Once Danielle started at St. Christopher's, they never saw each other at all, except for when they would walk by each other downtown. She was always with Lara Soto, and all these others really snobby princess-y but still hip with their black nail polish Catholic girls.

Janet would just look at her, thinking how she was all alone but Danielle was in this big group, and so that meant Danielle should be the one to come say hi to her. Only, Danielle never did.

***

Janet had been in 7-11 after Karate class buying some grape gum for the walk home when Danielle and Lara walked in. Janet had watched in shock as Bartles & Jaymes was slipped under denim. And she had gotten the nerve to confront Danielle, and Danielle had just walked away.

Janet was crying and kicking a pebble while she walked home. She shoved three pieces of purple Bubblicious in her mouth at once. She was remembering. Her and Danielle's secret hand shake, which was forty-six seconds long. The time they stoled her stepdad's Coors Light and put Lipton ice tea mix in it because they heard it made it taste good. Reading *Flowers In The Attic* together. The Ouija Board. How Danielle had walked all the way to her house the night her stepdad slapped her "by mistake", and slept over for three days.

Without Danielle in her life, Janet felt like a big gigantic jew pimple. Like a walking pimple. Like everyone was looking at her all the time. She was this weird thing that didn't fit anywhere. She was always bumped in the halls, so mondo in the way-mo. She'd eat really fast in a bathroom stall and sit in the library for the rest of lunch. She'd mope when she got home, and the more her parents tried to be nice to her, the more she loathed herself. She'd flop on her bed and stare at the ceiling, and couldn't believe how much slower time went without Danielle to talk to.

Evening fell, and Janet worked up the nerve to call Danielle. Or she couldn't bear the distance anymore. Either way, Danielle answered.

"Hullo?"

"Hey. Danny. It's Janet. And. I. Miss you and this sucks so hard and I can't take it anymore and I dunno why you want to be all Catholic now but I miss you so super bad and please don't hate me anymore and remember when we made up that whole dance to Rock Lobster? and I just whatever just miss you and I think you still have my favorite Guess jeans that you borrowed because I can't find them anywhere and I made out with Steve Wintersol and I need to talk to you about that and I am sorry I freaked out but I can't believe you are stealing from 7-11 they have cameras in there and what if you got busted do you know how much trouble you would get in? and mostly I am jealous that you are doing all this with Lara Soto and do you even miss me at all? and who have you made out with and have you smoked pot yet? I just miss you really so bad."

"I made out with Brodie Hanover."

Janet felt like she was slipping on her most favorite comfy sweater times a million. "Who's that? Is he dreamy?"

Danielle giggled. "Sooo dreamy. But he kisses weird."

"Like how?"

"I dunno. Like a lizard. He touched my boob under my bra though."

"Wait, what? Ohmigod."

"And yeah, I smoked pot two times but it didn't do anything."

Janet's heart sank. "You smoked pot without me? But we promised each other."

"Sor-ry"

"I smoked it too. Only once. And I didn't feel anything either. But we read that might happen, 'member?'" Things were going so perfectly. Janet didn't want to ruin it by admitting that without Danielle, all the fun of seeking out scandalous things to do had seeped out of her.

"Yup."

Then they just sat and listened to each other breathe for a while.

"Did you have your period yet?"

"No, silly. Gosh Janet, it hasn't been that long. Um. So. What are you doing tomorrow night? I'm babysitting around the corner from your house, and Brodie is gonna come over with Devon. Remember him?"

Devon was a dreamy St. Christopher's boy with a sideways haircut and an attitude.

"Yeah, that would be awesome."

Danielle called Janet as soon as she got the baby down. Janet grumbled an explanation to her already half passed out mom and went over, nervous and happy. When she walked in, they hugged, and even did their entire secret handshake. She still didn't understand Danielle's crispy bangs, but other than that, it was like nothing had ever changed.

Brodie and Devon showed up a half hour later. Brodie and Danielle started making out on the couch and so Devon and

Janet went and sat on the stairs and frenched for a while, tongues pinwheeling around each other. Devon reached inside her shirt and kind of flopped his hand over her bra, feeling her boobs, which were really not much more than nipples popped out like two mosquito bites.

Neither Janet nor Danielle really experienced peer pressure, ever. Because they wanted to try everything, know what everything was about, never look naive. They collected experiences like other girls collected Cabbage Patch Dolls.

Brodie hollered to Devon and he abruptly stopped kissing her, and walked briskly to the couch. Janet followed. Brodie and Devon kept walking and Danielle mouthed "come on" and grabbed Janet by the wrist. They all went out to the back porch, where Brodie produced a pipe, lighters and clove cigarettes for "covering the pot-smell," which he explained with an air of savoir-faire.

Danielle and Janet both acted nonchalant, like they always did, especially when doing something they were still unfamiliar with. They inhaled from the pipe three times each, and tried the delicious smelling clove cigarettes. The boys got bored and left. The girls felt vaguely paranoid that they were being rejected, but mostly, they were relieved to be with just each other. They grinned goofily and did their secret handshake again.

The pot had worked for both of them. They laughed hysterically at the air, and ate cheddar cheese, and listened to Abbey Road on the Wilkinsons' stereo. When the grownups got home, Janet snuck quickly out the back door and gate and waited around the corner for Danielle to get paid and walk over. The time alone in the quiet smalltown night made her thoughtful.

When Danielle finally arrived, she giggled once, and then fell silent too. They walked towards home slowly. After four blocks they plopped down together on the curb without discussion, shivering and happy. They stared up at the swirling stars, which glowed like dying ember match heads in the giant black ashtray of the sky.

POEMS

M A Y B E

this doesn't want to be a song of suffering or luxury
it just wants
just want to be
maybe me is enough

maybe these legs young and sturdy
used to run through open fields unending
riddled with lightning fat as nebuchadnezzar's thighs
and more plentiful than breath
artfully dodging electricity
like freeway traffic
that entire summer of eleven
when it hot rained every day in deep green
and sun hid for forty minutes
the vermont air a thick mist of mosquitoes
and i was more bites than fresh skin
even on palms
and it was then i discovered the violent femmes

maybe my first memory of letters forming words
that wormed meaning inside me
was *poem for flora* by nikki giovanni

and so maybe i express too many sentiments
with torah references

maybe i have danced until my feet would bleed
for over half my life
but every year
that percentage is lessening

maybe i used to daydream
on top of the old brown volare
inside the frank lloyd wright invention

and maybe i attempted to use cinderblocks

to build a stairway to heaven
due to early exposure to led zeppelin
i only made it as far as the top of the carport
but i was closer there

and the stars in my sphere
were clear enough to whisper to back then
before the chains came
and so maybe that's how i still know them

and maybe i never found a place to belong
and still search
with my soul
held out before me
like a flashlight in both hands

maybe ocean and cold blue
with slick metallic fish
makes sense to me like planets and addition

and turning
is physics
 in pale pink
and muscles
that answer
with quick precision
simple and significant

and
i am the child of dusty jung and smoke and laughter and style
and
pens and hunting and pecking and october country
and
jumping on beds
and

maybe in june i left the window with no screen mistakenly open
in my room and the tiniest starling flew in and hid in my closet
and i didn't know until it flew out while i was asleep

i thought i was dreaming

maybe i put my heart on my sleeve
and astoret on my spine to remind myself of things

and maybe i cry when i hear music
because it trips the wire on my internal chemistry

and maybe if you look too long
you'll notice the holes
and you can watch the atoms dance
and remember that we are just bundles of energy

and
maybe i will be alright if i can just keep breathing

and
maybe i have tried to break my own bones
just to see if i could do it

its hard to be human

this package is savage and flawed

just collected wetness and hot whispers

vulnerable and easy to attack

a skinsack of slippery tubes fluid and skeleton
and underneath
nothing

and it makes me want to hold everyone
and i say *i love you* a lot

and i mean it
really
earnestly
yearningly

i am burning up with refracted passion

i am ablaze with amazement
aching with the taking in
of all these little pieces
of majesty
and beauty
and frailty

this
just wants
just want to be
maybe me is enough
with my soul
held out before me
like a flashlight
in both hands

FREE, FALL

pluck the irises
from my eyes
the bloom
from my cheeks

dislodge tongue
from jaw
like the errant strawberry
it yearns to be

when will
pearls all tumble?
when will
the taught tautness slack?

define:
crux?
nexus?

lie in wait under flaws
and rickety skeleton
lie in wait behind lush
and respiration

unfold crossed limbs
transcend the panic of open
pulse: quicken then slow

trust beyond faith
to the flipside of
complacent

bravery
proves its essential mettle when tested

and only in that moment

SPECIAL

now, i cannot tell you his name, not even what
breed, but i can tell you he was huge and tan
and curly-furred, can tell you how his dog-
strong back felt under my miniature hand, and
how autumn early-evenings, my father and i
ventured the three-quarter block to pacheco
elementary school where i would roll around
the blacktop, resplendent in my standard-
issue   white-with-red-and-blue-stripes-roller
skates, de rigueur for any five year old girl in
nineteen seventy-eight, and sometimes, curly-
tan would be there with his owner, an old man
in a navy blue greek fisherman's cap, and
curly tan, he was dog enough for me to grab
on to his leash, let him drag me, gliding over
hopscotch and four-square demarcations like
i couldn't be fenced in. llke i was somebody
special.

now, i cannot tell you what it felt like in a father-
heart to watch such an event unfolding, but i
can tell you how he made his arms a cradle for
my skate-heavy, clanking-ankled, body, how
he spirited me home, laid me on my bed and
unlaced the skates, how my face bled, can tell
you how my mother cleaned that burning, i
fled the scene by falling asleep, curly-tan had
been pulling me, it was blissful until wheel
kissed rock, until i faceplanted into asphalt,
until he had his back to me, kept right on
running, how i covered ground like that until
synapses, at long last, snapped to attention,
until brain sent word to hand, how holding
on was not helping. such echoes, strained
beggings, across blacktop, my father's voice:
let go

MONTANA DE ORO

we are the girls with the cheesegrater hearts
wet red nicks inflicted with each involuntary beat

with driveway spikes for teeth
piercing our lips
backing out every word uttered
with oedipal proportioned inevitability

we are the girls
with timebomb tongues
counting down until others
duck and cover
unable to contain the runaway train
of our freightweighted force of nature

with pocketfuls of shiny shards
with palmfuls of question marks
with bellyfuls of crackling chrysalis glittering

we are the girls
anointed in snake oil
we didn't covet

and now are we running
breathless
from screaming at joshua trees
in the rain
to make clean what was tainted
praying to be redeemed:
in/clemency

we are the girls exquisite in our comprehension
of excruciate
we spill love
we are leaking transmissions
from each duct

yet
for every breath we
ponder reversing
for every moment insurmountable
we are tenfold beholden grateful
awestruck
at the vast and delicate delectation
of this particular and precious and tenuous existence
we are bursting at the seams
innocent criminals
teeming with rubies

we make way

any helena will tell you
consider the orchid amputated and atrophying in glass
notice the skinned bloodball of discarded mink:
it is the nature of our species
to destroy what it desires
to consume
to violate and take
what it deems beauty

we make way

we are the girls trapped in concrete
only knowing there is a snowglobe inside
a memory floating in pale grace

a place where the bottom of the sea
has heaved its own tectonics
and nudged up through the surface of the earth
in all its sedimentary splendor

it is triumph despite the unbearable gravity of being
we make way
with pocketfuls of shiny shards
with palmfuls of question marks
with bellyfuls of crackling chrysalis glistening,

glittering.

L I E   D O W N   B E S I D E   Y O U

when i lie down beside you,
your fingertips whisper to me
secrets that you don't even know you know
your touch belies your desire
like livewire,

sparks fly when i lie down beside you

and lord knows – i am yours
spread me open, unfold me
like ouija-
without speaking i convey supernatural communication
like-
clandestine alphabet beating beneath my chest
like-
this way means yes
like-
never having to second-guess
like-
prophetic text made manifest

like rapture, light crackles when i lie down beside you

press against me-
i am strong enough to receive the message you're delivering
believe in the taste of my devotional
notice the way i melt for you
let every tear be dripping elixir
let your sweet exhalation fill me
let there be laying of your hands on my body
memorize my topography
listen to the whisper of my history

i am physical science when i lie down beside you

play archeologist to my landscape

there are verbs needing to be unearthed
truths traveling circuitous routes through my veins
i hold all of your answers rattling in my wrists
and revelation with bliss remixed glistening in my lips
and match disclosure chance for chance with the dancing in my
hips
i can uncurl my defenses if you let me
lay the manuscript of your meaning at your feet
discern your direction with the cleft of intimate wish held out
before me

i am your diviner when i lie down beside you

i am your trail of astralprojected bread crumbs
preternatural cartography
spirit guide in the flesh
unwind my dna and view the blueprint of my destiny
and then rest with me
breathless but easy
set your cares in the nautilus of my ear
where they will mingle with the whisper of eternal rolling ocean
i want to hear
i will hide them like sunken treasure
and
they will be there within
whether you ever retrieve them

waves crash bright when i lie down beside you

you riptide into me
let me love you
hand to mouth cheek to cheek speak in tongues on my skin
you are delicious beyond recognition
i give in to precious potential
like-
constellations weep in appreciation of our creation
like-
spheres wax harmonic
like-
everything spinning in unison

like-
we are more than our human machination
and molecular combinations and
we are mysteries constantly unriddling

i am particular night sky when i lie down beside you

take me
and make me your astrology
plot your path by my best star
i offer it like open palm
like conviction
like undeniable truth
like specific blessing
like honest
like you inside me
like lightning striking twice
every single time

so take me like
i am meteorology
like
i am metaphysics
like poetry

take me like i am

i am

i am

when i lie down beside you

creekside,
she whispered to the sycamore, eucalyptus.
knelt to the whistling water.
prayed. waited.

three days later she awakened,
blanketed over with bark, leaves
covering her eyes.
she knew what to do.

with a rock, lobbed off
locks of hair.
buried it beneath moss and lichen.
sacrificed.
conjured.
walked deeper into the green.
gathered these brittle tree pieces.

she might have magicked much,
but fashioned a girl out of it.

hands, branching from rickety arms.
feet, rooting in worm-darkness.
head, nodding heliotropist.

ever reaching eight-directioned,
arching and undulating and locked
to one spot.

i know nothing of the love of man.

the center of me, mysterious
and swirling, secreted from
intrepid fingers, fastened,
impenetrable.

ears,

flooded with minnows and bubbling river.

eyes,
blinking back brown rings.

all rushing movement
trapped and stationary.

and how shall i be anything but grateful
to she, who,
born barren-wombed, dreamed a daughter hard enough to
(single-handedly) burst her into existence?

and how shall i do anything but rage
against she, who
selfishly tricked me into taking in
oxygen
(and carbon dioxide,)
half woman
(half kindling,)
solitary and unending?

have i no choice in the matter?

a headful of possibilities,
only made to burn?

LUCKY

Today, everything is grotesquely portentous,
and still am I complicated and flawed.
I, misshapen darkness.
It makes me want to escape,
makes me want to hide under ten thousand layers,
makes me feel I was meant for burkas and beatings,
and through some cosmic anomaly
had the good fortune to be born

american.

I apologetically robe myself in the cloak of only-night-time.
Veil my indecent face with the liquor you drink.
Pray nobody looks too close and notices
the wrongness
I embody.

4 3 9

at this 4:39 a.m.
i am cognizant alert and all predatory magic
luxuriating in this slip of pre
time
the right
before
favored by
divers rodeo riders ticklish children roller coaster aficionados
and
yours
truly
everything only theoretical
and delicious mystery
i like it right here
cushioned on clouds of
to-be-announced
i am tasting anticipation like maple still locked in trunk
it is nearly perfect
more branches and sunlight than roots and earth
nearly perfect
it is not yet your actual mouth
just the promise of

D A I Y E N U

had you-i been given but seconds in this unreal reality,
and the ten-thousand things not made themselves known to
me-you,
daiyenu,

had the ten-thousand things made themselves known to me-
you,
and your-my blood not thudded circuitously, stubbornly,
daiyenu,

had your-my blood thudded circuitously, stubbornly,
and these atoms not stayed gathered into matter as me-you,
daiyenu,

had these atoms stayed gathered into matter as me-you,
and you-i not been born earthly entity,
daiyenu,

had you-i been born earthly entity,
and these lungs not breathed me-you,
daiyenu,

had these lungs breathed me-you,
and you-i not strengthened from struggling,
daiyenu,

had you-i strengthened from struggling,
and the time-space web not caught me-you,
daiyenu,

had the time-space web caught me-you,
and you-i not made manifest believed-in possibility,
daiyenu,

had you-i made manifest believed-in possibility,
and never felt faith inside me-you,

daiyenu,

had you-i felt faith inside me-you,
and not lost ego-identity,
daiyenu,

had you-i lost ego-identity,
and not detached from a conceptually separate me-you,
daiyenu,

had you-i detached from a conceptually separate me-you,
and never found inner tranquility,
daiyenu,

had you-i found inner tranquility,
and never let angel-death tongue-kiss me-you,
daiyenu,

had you-i let angel-death tongue-kiss me-you,
and not answered with reciprocity,
daiyenu,

had you-i answered with reciprocity,
and not still vibrated energy for eternity,
had you-i been given but seconds in this unreal reality,
had it all been arbitrary,
had it all been but a word,
a breath,
a blink,
a touch,
a grace,
a pulse,
a truth,
daiyenu,
daiyenu,

daiyenu.

12 DAYS

you are beautiful in your occlusion,
how can i not want to unlock you?
i am a safecracker
listening at keyholes
for the other pin to drop.
picking at clasp like
irresistible scab.

you are beautiful in your pollution,
the way smog creates
the most breathtaking
sunsets.

you are perfection in your flaws,
off-kilter
and odd-
number
i can't help but double,

break
even,
with all of my shortcomings,
resolving everything,

and you are re-doubly beautiful in resolution.

you are beautiful in your confusion,
gloriously juxtaposed on the backdrop
of my single-minded
decisiveness.

meanwhile,
i'm moving mountains
that haven't yet found you,
to arrive at your side
in the still of the night,

cloaked in glowing obsidian,
one atom loosed,
wrapped in radioactive
alabaster ice satin static-
charged

like electric,
like accused,

like irreducible truth:

you knew this
before
you knew this
before

you knew me .
you undo me
like knots,
honest you do.
you send me

terrified likeletters,
and i smile.

i am reconciled
to this newness.

from the southwest cusp of my bed
to north star far,

tattoo
ptolemaeic astronomic cartography
across my body.
unbox this constellation.

for better or worse,
there is an epicenter
to my rickety richter universe.

you render me trembling
unprecedented.

and you
are beautiful in your frustration.

i will make you come

around.

I OO LIVES

i reckon
i'm a destined
perfectionist
      when it comes
to
      making love
to you,
'cause 100 lives
is not even enough time
    for me to love you
    all the ways i'm intending to.
why?
because you're you.
because of the way you mmmmm
because you
    climb me like i'm a spiral staircase,
    savoring each twist and curve,
    deserving each awakened nerve ending.
bending around the beginning until you've unwound
back around me again.
and i wanna touch a man who feels like that.
i wanna touch a man who feels as much as you do.
i wanna feel you.
i wanna feel you like my palms are mouths
      and your skin is oxygen.
feel you like my fingertips are devout eyes
      and your flesh is the messiah.
feel you like dreams need an unconscious mind to reside in.
feel you like something so right and exciting,
      there's no wasting time on fright or deciding.
feel you like
dance needs song, weak needs strong, right needs wrong,
      for a long time.
and then i'm gonna devour you.
'cause i wanna devour a man who tastes like you do.
i wanna taste a man who devours the way you do.

for hours, i wanna taste you.
i wanna taste you like i'm the desert,
and you're the pouring rain.
taste you like pleasure needs pain.
taste you like i'm gonna make you attain nirvana.
taste you like i don't wanna waste a single drop.
i hope there's no place you need to be,
because me?
i'm gonna taste you like i ain't never gonna stop.
until you pop and then flop on the drenched bed exhausted.
and that's not it.

i'm gonna let you in.
'cause i wanna receive a man who goes as deep as you do,
i wanna receive you.
i wanna receive you like i'm the seashore,
          and you're the sea.
receive you like i got the lock,
          and you got the key.
receive you like i'm some secret military airplane
          hanger and you're the stealth bomber jet,
receive you like the final payment on a long standing debt,
receive you like the return
of that certain person
you just weren't
able to forget,
but it's that fucked-up-destiny feeling,
'cause i know this is the first time we've met,
(at least in this lifetime.)
and if this sublime crime
comes to an end
before i'm satisfied,
i will know that once i've died
and gone to the next place,
i will stand face to face
with my creator
and state that
the greater the bliss the further the fall from grace,
and beg that same creator
to return me
to this earthly

place,

and you will be here too.
and we will recognize each other
like delicious déjà vu.
like we always do.
like we're supposed to.
why?
'cause,
100 lives
is not even enough time
    for me to love you
      all the ways i'm intending to…

i reckon
i'm a destined
perfectionist
    when it comes
to
    making love
to you.

I F

(oh, how cruel this world can be,
yet full of comfort and splendor)

today, your heart grew
redundant as a cultist,

dreaming of pyramids
in giza.

started
thinking of these united states,
weeping for murdered lambs and chickadees.

chest, heavy with branch davidian vessels
pumping jonestown koolaid.

nobody would dare to call you
undedicated.

nobody could doubt your commitment.

i appreciate your constant restraint.
the incessant battle between impulse and control.

the synapses dancing right through the window of your
beautiful attic.

if i could stop this planet from spinning,
lay my hands upon your skull,
bring ease and reassurance,
i would raise my arms like atlas
and brake the rotation,
to make a pocket of time
for us to breathe,
just breathe
in.

T I T U L A R

now...

some of you might not believe this,
'cause it's fucking pathetic,
but it's true.
and some of you might get confused
trying to understand
what kinda man
i have been known in the past to pursue-
but-
i believe
there is a seed
of something wise,
some insight inside it,
if i can find it,
so try and
follow this through.

before you have a chance to misconstrue the issue,
lemme just tell you
that this is a poem about
a conversation about...

...boobs.

my boobs.

there's not much to discuss,
we're talkin' a-cups,
but they're mine,
and i like 'em just fine.

so,
i'm sitting in a car with my ex,
(now we're just friends,
i mean we broke up years ago,)

and he goes,
(mind you, between crooning the lyrics of
just the way you are by billy joel,)

he goes:
ya know, i like your boobs better
when you're on the pill and they're
all swollen from the hormones.

allow me to state at this juncture
that the structure
of this story has not been altered one iota
to fill some quota
for the sake of poetry.
seriously!
he actually said this shit to me while singing
just the way you are by billy joel.
and, in describing how he liked these titties to be,
he actually used the word *swollen*.

this guy, who thinks he's all hippy,
all vegetarian granola earthy,
actually thinks it matters to me
how he prefers my titties to be,
and he is suggesting that i engorge them artificially
with the birth control pill,
aka bcp,
aka hormone therapy.
excuse me?

excuse me?

so i go,

listen, honey,
these titties don't belong to you, they belong to me!
and they are currently protruding from my body
exactly how my god intended them to be!
and- you know what?

104

these babies may be just a cups-
but these muthafuckas are perky!
and they will be, well past thirty!
they stand at attention
24-7...

...wait, wait, hold up,
you know what?
that point is moot,
'cause my intention
is to mention
that your perception
of my worth physically
doesn't mean shit to me!
what?
do i need more breast meat
like some mutant-deformo poultry
to be shipped to kfc?
are you kidding me?
umm...i am trusting
you don't want to go to deep into the size discussion,
let's not rush into that one too fast,
because, uh, she who laughs last...

...well, i'll leave the rest to your imagination.

the point of my poetic exploration
of this conversation
is me, venting my unending frustration,
in hopes of imparting at least a partial explanation
of the situation
i am facing due to the limitation
some guy is placing with his dissertation
on my current physical manifestation,
and his recommendation
that through artificial fetal gestation
i trick these boobies into swollen and confused
pseudo food
containers!

it makes my brain hurt just to consider it.

by the way-

post script:

while my boobies were all swollen
with the hormones of the bcp,
there was this constant ache
that made it to painful
to touch them,
let alone be playful with them.

and who's that fun for?

nobody!

not anybody!

definitely not me!

owww!

so screw you, dude.
and screw your swollen titty fantasy.

my boobies,
my body,
my beauty.

newsflash:
it's not for you, it's for me.

me!

NATURE

(i will not be silent)
(i speak on your behalf)
(messy and violent)

      i cannot mutter my way
      out from under this weight of frustration

when a person is kept from her true nature through repression
her essence will manifest by any means necessary

when a human has been deprived of her own instincts
like a dandelion forcing its own growing to shoot through
cracked concrete

life force
will reach
will not be denied or suppressed
will express and use whatever it is able to access
to best estimate its destiny
unconsciously

this
is emancipation through proclamation
because
      i cannot mutter my way
      out from under this weight of frustration
that lays heavy on our gender

and even though the constant fight makes me tired
still
it is required of me
i was made for raging
i am simply not equipped to keep a stiff upper lip and chin up
i was built for blasting
this outcry is my calling

and i was once child
and now am i woman
and my mind was shrouded
and how i couldn't
understand the nature of temptation to swim in the dark pool of
psyche
raised in a society that maligns impulse   intuition
instinct
for one simple reason:

these qualities are feared by the autocrat
because if released
they would undoubtedly supply the marginalized with
heretofore unseen power and grounding

to wit
the oppressor doesn't want the woman in touch with her sixth
sense
'cause he's scared shitless of her as it now stands

imagine if her channel was open

imagine if her prowess was loosed

so what does the lost womanchild do?

          she reaches she craves she holds tea party séances
          plays with ouija boards obsesses over ghosts and non-
          existent mystical animals chants bloody mary in the
mirror
          hears voices like an army of joan of arcs drowns like a
fleet
          of ophelias in the trying to read boys' minds and now for
her
          next trick attempts to make herself simply disappear one
denied
          meal at a time just to be in control of any single aspect
her life then

silences the rising scream inside with any prescription or
bottle or plant
she can get her hand on
which is simple
because it's
exactly
what the ones on top want
she is doing their job for them now
that's how subversive this
cycle is

she dances with reckless abandon hand in hand with abject
abandonment
she wants to howl at the moon fall to her knees and be
woman

*and what of all of this inherent tendency and urgent longing and
innate knowledge?*

she dreams of ways that blades could unleash the coax that
lives in her bones
crawls on her
skin

it is an unoriginal sin we unintentionally commit
it is a constant covering up and simultaneous longing to reveal
it is a constant numbing up and simultaneous longing to feel

it is real

and if she could halt the voices for even the length of one breath
the sky inside her mind might open
and her very flesh would buzz with eternal collective memory

at least she could love herself
at least she could see her beauty
at least she could believe in remembering

and when the terrible hard wired tirade finally abated

a new
clear and
focused voice
would speak
like a hand
and guide her
from inside her

maybe it's not too late
pray forgotten goddesses
haven't given up on us just yet

we can commit to resurrecting lost sisters
we can make offerings of more life
rather than any more sacrifice
instant isis and impromptu ishtar
essential esther and ad hoc astoret

we cannot forget

we can silence the insidious intentional static
that keeps us from hearing our
actual inside

      i cannot mutter my way
      out from under this weight of frustration

it's time to get to the real quiet

so we can finally

scream

WORD TO THE WHY?S

do you think i have a choice?
why do you think god gave me this voice?
just to make random noise?
even though i've always known,
the more i write, the more i realize
the words aren't even mine.
i am just a channel
for those outside of time
to use
to travel through if they so choose
(and so often they do.)
i speak to you,
but they convey the message
(which i have sworn not to misconstrue.)
i am an internal shapeshifter.
eternal uplifter.
whether you see it as a gift or a curse makes no difference.
for better or worse, that's what i was put on earth to do.

now, here's what i remember
about heaven, or the next level, or the netherworld, or
whatever name you prefer:
before we get to earth,
before we arrive, alive,
through the tunnel of our mother to our birth,
we're hanging out in that other place
and we decide our own fate.
we're hanging out with god,
or the universal consciousness, or the creator, or
whatever you prefer to name her,
and we decide the paths and challenges of our own lives.
but check it out:
it all seems really groovy from up there,
its just like watching a movie from up there.
there's lessons we're sent to this planet to learn
and god lets us plan it on our own terms.

0 0 0

and sometimes god will say things, like,
me damn! you sure you can handle it all?

and we're all cocky like we stand fifty feet tall
strong, can conquer any wall,
'cause up there we know we can never truly fall,
except into the arms of our creator,
'cause remember, we got to state our terms.
but here's why it burns.
here's the bitter eternal truth,
the worm inside eve's fruit:
once we get to earth,
we have to start at birth, anew,
as helpless bumbling humans.
we can't remember the plan, understand?
that's part of the lesson.
our memories are stripped clean, see what i mean?
god has to keep us guessing once we get here
so that when we experience what we chose, it's crystal clear.
we can't be exposed to the before or else in our mortal bodies,
we might not walk through any door.

so now you know the score.
whether you are here as a queen or a whore,
when you think things can't get any worse
and it seems like you're coming apart at the seams,
just remember that you're the one who schemed these
schemes,
and everything is as it should be, and everything's ok,
and i am simply here so that you can hear this message today,
'cause at the end of it all what else can you say
but that which you know to be true
'cause you've seen it with your own two eyes?

and that's my word to the
W
H
Y?s.

COME

       i will come
like a flashback finally slack and unraveling
like intaken breath
like your best guess
like warm air caresses cold flesh
i am resting intentionally in the parentheses
of your future-tense memory

       i will come
like karma
like déjà vu
the dance you've always known the steps to
i am specifically meant to directly address you
and my best fantasy is your smile

       I'll come
from
around the corner of your mind
out of the blue
out of left field
the snatched tatter of a dream
that seemed real
worth remembering
the other side of the membrane
separating everything from everything

i am the whisper from the ghost in the machine

i am the promise from a fickle god you thought forgot you
i am the feast on the laden table
ready
legs buckling

i am the *what if*

the obsolete pattern

shattered
unspiraled and unspooling

i am on the one hand
and
i am the other answer undone
i am gathering your crackled crumbs
of heartdust and wetting them with
my own blood

i am the fixed zippers in your malfunctioning wrists
i am buttoning the lip of your suicide note with kisses
i am the manifestation of never-thought-existed
the message hidden in the backwards vinyl of your death wish

i am the payoff for 11,011 days of alienation
i am the holding
i am the release
i am what will wrap around you
and i am brave enough to
make *yes* and
my arrival is predestined
no matter how as-yet imperceptible
i am breathless with the building portent

and i am terrified
confounded
and blinded
despite this

           i will come
see the tumbling puzzle pieces falling at my feet
forming synergetic street
i am fate's servant
following
faithful
fervent

i am for you
all your glass-bottled messages come rolling up my shore

114

all your wishes drifting inexplicably to my star

this is me versus monolith
unable to avoid what is blatant
i can't not read the smoke signals billowing from your burning
desire
can't not translate the morse encoded in your heart beat
can't not finger the frail brail in your subtle-bodied veins
and
wait

     i will come
like
bass thumping up 111th street
like thunder rumbling
from 111 paces
like anticipation

     i will come
like
pins and needles
a stomachful of butterflies
paroxysmal thighs
stifled cries
eyes looking up and inside lids

     i will come
like
vehement agonizing beauty

     i will come
like
pulse
throb
wonderment

     i will come
at the 11th second
when you least expect it

         i will come
when pathetic misdirection
causes you to
at long last
abandon
self-fulfilling prophecies
and
lose your taste for
mapmaking
and
urges you to
throw down
the accordioned paper web of blue and red

and then
when you are
empty-handed
eye-opened
readied

i will arrive

make no mistake

like a chorus of a thousand
hallelujahs

         i will come

BADLAND BETWEEN

if i knew you from adam,
i could tell myself from eve.
(you can have your precious rib back.)

gladly split atomic,
ricocheted four states away.

here is you:
permitted behind my wheel,
careening back and forth,
one frontier to another.

here is you:

it is raw power here,
more beautiful there.

this is erosion.

the whys and wherefores
of intake.

we are twinned watery graves;
try each other on for size.

this is the badland between us.

uninhabitable,
treacherous,
our hearts, always burning like bridges.

here is you:
theorizing on reverse reincarnation.
singing with mccartney.
dreaming of backjumping into a new suit of lennon-skin,
fragile and medicated.

later, your face will screw up into sobs.
i'll press your head against my breast,
envy your safety,
taste my desire to cry.
think of much
i would smuggle across your border.

i've no taste for negotiations.

i gather spilled guts,
tie them into their previous knots.

my heart flops out regardless,
only all distorted,
like
remember me
like
forget i said that
like
forgive me

WHEN THE LIGHT WENT OUT,

when the light went out,

there was a burst of breeze behind the curtain.

when the light went out,

smell of roses, clove, cardamom.

when the light went out,

weight fell upon my chest and was lifted off my neck.

a feather landed.

a flurry of dirt on the sparkling earth surface.

a caught breath,
a cat listened,
a wave stood mid-crash,
god turned,
and turned again,
and then,

the moon continued its orbit.

I DO IT AGAIN

you're my crash course
in eschatology

heart sinking
so fast
it's almost floating
flying

funny how falling feels just like rising
once you learn to close your eyes right

the closest i ever getto emancipation from shackle-gravity
comes from succumbing to its thrust completely

careening
head over heels
until the slap of concrete humiliates
the mortality right back into me

     i tongue the ground so much
     because i can trust it

     there is comfort in the reliable fact
     of
     the hit the dirt again again
     like clockwork

addicted to the machine
fingering your socket
of electroshock heart
just for the assurance

the redolent scent of burning flesh
the lightning jolt
bolting up this pulsating
persistent

living carcass

the incontrovertible solace
that comes
certain
with bearing the full frontal
brunt of my
inconsequence

you make me this inadequate

you're the vortex i lay my weary head
through

kisses like depth charges
nosedives i never decompress from
lips laced with magnets and hemlock

i am
displaced person
immaterial spirit
homeless

you took up residence in the pit of the middle of me
heavy and pressing
my mundane limbs give out

face down
i burrow in earth
smell soil sweet
and go unnoticed until the abject invisibility grows unbearable
again
and then...

and then...

and then...

SOULCAR

I wanna park
my soul's car
on a raked driveway,
slanted
dramatically
above the home
below,
so
that when I open
all four
of my soul's car doors,
they fall fast forward
towards the house,
almost double-jointing in their hinges,
impinging on nerves almost,
and I will park my car
on a sunny warm
day
and that way,
the doors can stay open like that,
bent almost back,
for hours and hours.

My soul's car needs some cross-ventilation.

Maybe even some buzzing bees
or
pollen from trees
will pass through on the recently (temporarily) unimpeded
breeze.

I need to get my soul's car's inside cleaned!

     (I will keep my e-brake on
      so I don't roll forward and crash the garage.)

A falling forward provocation.
A trajectory in suspended animation.
A study in concentration.

I am orbiting my genetic home in my soul's car
and the farther I drive away, the closer I arrive each day,
for reality is curved,
and orbits' paths always return
          to the beginning,
always return to the burn,
always return to the birth.

So I open all four of my soul's car's windows,
crank the e-brake back as far as it goes,
let the door slam open so my soul is exposed,

and freeze,
mid-flight,
in an
angle
of
repose.

HOT OF YOUR DRAW

and i
i am accelerating

essentially the best of me is wrestling in ecstasy with the rest of me which intentionally represses the blessing to the extent of detested resentment it's a testament to the flesh's sixth sense and propensity for unrelenting destruction and i wonder will i survive or will i be rent asunder crumbling undone thunder unraveling battling demons till i'm beaten down reasonless and the reason i'm feeling like speaking this thesis is weakness that bleeds my soul out to you hold out till you turn blue it's worth it to deserve this wicked honesty

honestly
you've got to be wanting the drama to even start this with me

weaving through and fingering realness with impunity

i enter at my own risk knowing this isn't the brightest idea
but desire overrides all other thoughts

when the hot of your drawing unlocks me

and i
i am accelerating

you are just hands
and knowing that
neither harms nor warms me
bears terrible precious little significance
in this particular instance

you are the leaf flipped around the windshield wiper of my
existence
and i
i am accelerating
you wrap over ever harder

wiggling in the wind
holding on for dear life

you are just hands
you are the 10,000 things on every inch of me
and i am thinking
about each of you

i am feeding back
rattling your amp
impossibly

my body responds automatic unconsciously
when the hot of your drawing unlocks me

the want of your clawing's what mocks me
leaving me responsible for a constant opening unfolding of
urgency
lay myself down on the altar, play my part in the legacy

i am mute i am chemical i am concentric circles
looping through each other
little deaths in both directions

i am silently writhing in spite of myself
i am a first prize science project
i'm the picture of health
i am stimulus and response on display
i am as natural as the day is long
as predictable as kittens
right as rain and sunrise
overcome by pleasure delectable
edging unbearable
tear at your own my hair forget to exhale type of excitement
and

you are just hands
you wear your competitive streak
like bloodstained fingers
a killer smile and a file up your sleeve

planning long-term for the jailbreak when you're
caught red-palmed
hot
of your wanting
unlocking me

i am winning at the game i didn't want to play

and i
i am accelerating

when the hot of your drawing unlocks me

and the plot of this haunting won't stop me
because this longing is stronger than gravity
because i want it like drops of rain want sea
like i'm magnetized, hogtied by moonbeams
you're the 10,000 things all up on me
when the
hot
of your drawing
unlocks me

IF I COULD BE YOUR

i'm a
reluctant delilah
tryng to be right
fantasizing
about what i
could do
to you
how it would play out
wondering what would happen
if i could be your
cleopatra

the attraction
would be palpable
if i was capable

if i could let go and whisper
through midnight-lighted leaves
believe in things easily
like the sanctity of secrets
ride life like a swing to and fro
if i could be your
cleopatra

i'd free you from within my capture
i'd be teaching you the real meaning of reaching rapture

take a stand within your tricky pyramid
see through your scheme
dream this into near-reality
with sheer will

and
if i could
stand still

and simply exist

resist all this feeding of this sickness within
which continues its plague
with fake hunger

for something

underneath this skin

is a maze of veins.
i'd drain them by praying
'til the day
i went blue in the face
if i thought it meant salvation

under this skin

is the indigo depth charge
starless night
full of wishes
with no event horizon
rising
like snow in reverse
cursed into oblivion
that i'm sitting in
continuing to ruminate on twists of fate
like
what if i could be your cleopatra?

but even this gets even more twisted
when i contemplate my state
because
i'm a
reluctant delilah
stricken with
the gift of exquisite manipulation
which i've taken vows against
now i drape loneliness over my chest
a lead smock

trying to block unwanted stimulation
trying to duck under the radar of your amazing radiation
protecting my vitals
from your x-ray ways of seeing inside of me
only
i'm the one climbing on the table
for examination
while your hands leave trails
of radioactive finger prints
glistening
i'm beginning to be
a supernatural crime scene
i'm all glow stick-y lime green

look at me
your touch shows all over the whole of me
trespassing
transgressions
i'm a plutonium road map
traversing within my skin,
brimming with opacity
that lastingly
juxtaposes
your luminescence

and the essence

i'm still alone in your presence
second-guessing whether i should break this vow
and if so
how

and if now is like
no other time like the present
then i guess
it stands to reason
that this is what it seems it is

part pathetic
part glorious

this story's so old
it's been told
until it's worn holes
in its pages from
mouths stating it

it is all seven stages of enlightenment
twisted into one simple perfect kiss
that lies in wait
behind
my
delilah lips
that wish they were pasted
to the face of the she
the she
who appears in your dreams

and they would be
if i could be
your
cleopatra

PRETTY TALK

case # 34-263
intensity vs. dignity
dead center of winter
i testify:

you and i
snuck into the theatre on christopher street
(how stupid were they to give us both our own set of keys)
after drinking ourselves silly at the back fence
you
on cold-buffalo-winter-type libations
all manly and shit
always rolling rock/guinness/jd if you were in a hurry
i don't remember what i was drinking
but about you
i remember everything
like the knit cap that said *dolomite*
and was from an actual mine
where the actually mined
the actual substance dolomite
you were that cool without even trying
and i remember your little round wire glasses
and how your last name was a verb and a noun
like mine
and when the bars closed at 4:00
ready for more
fingers all freezing and stumbly we'd unlock the theatre door
plop down right in the lobby
we were so full of 20-year-old balls
we didn't even bother to hide from the passersby
light up a bowl
read our favorite shepard and bukowski
to each other
proud of the sound
of how passionate righteous loud
our own voices could be

and then when we'd leave
we'd eventually go home
back to our place in brooklyn heights
where we were roommates
always acted like we never expected anything to happen
and then when we'd fuck
you never had your glasses on
and you were blind without them
i used to love staring up into that vacuous cow eye gaze
so oddly placed upon your brilliant face
and always
right after you came
while you were still inside me
you'd find your glasses
and put them on
blinking me into focus
and i really fucking liked that
and

you never said you loved me
god only knows if you ever did
just a fuck buddy who liked talking pretty with me

case # 17-256
lust vs. subversiveness
dead center of summer
i testify:

you and i
snuck into the walk-in fridge
downstairs in the just-below-harlem jazz bar we both worked in
it was too damn hot
everything
catching your scent when you went past me and i'd be wet in a
nanosecond
we couldn't help it
we fucked up against racks of zucchini and cabbages
squishing squash
and when my eyes finally shot open to watch the door
i caught sight of the slaughtered lamb

skinned just minutes before
by the hateful haitian chef i loved more than life
like a daddy
fate made her my sister by placing her in there
rachel
hebrew for lamb
both of us sacrificed on the altar of desire that night
as i took you inside me
and at 4 a.m. when the bar finally closed
we'd both have an after-work drink
bacardi limón and coke
(which was another thing you taught me)
and we'd squeeze like 10 pieces of lemon into each glass
and you'd speak to me in spanish
and i'd reply in my fucked up spanish
and then we'd stumble out- turning opposite corners
and i'd ride the 9 train
all the way home alone
and

you told me you loved me about a million times
god only knows if you ever did.
just a fuck buddy who liked talking pretty with me

case # 26-348
you'd make things so complicated
i'd get so frustrated
all i could do is cry

case # 4-13
you'd scream at me
to stop psychoanalyzing
everything

2-5
you'd lie
and tell me you were single

89
you were

133

terrified of my passion

11
you'd
leave me hanging

7
you'd let me down

3
you'd stare at me
a broken heap on the floor
and be at a loss for how to proceed
it never occurred to you
to hold me

i'm running in circles
looking for a loophole
i'm trying to be tried for prior uncomprehended crimes
and leave with a scot-free rap sheet this time
i want to make your obtuse angle bend in to spiritual acuity
some part of me believes
if i can solve it for you and me
than all the chains break
and i walk out of this prison
but i find you infinitely compelling
you
you emotionally distant motherfucking man
your kisses crash instantly
into that rift of what nobody can give to me
but i can't not want it
and if i could figure out how

i'd end this poem right now.

THIS PRECISE DESIRE

each night, discover him anew,
buried in blue fluid,
face-up, and supine, and trawl him
toward the shore.

on the packed sand,
wipe away the wet,
careful-palmed.

thumb open his lids
gentler than breath.
wait, patient, for eyes to flicker
into recognition.

fingerpart familiar lips.

watch in wonder while
he remembers breathing.

ache with adoration for his rise-and-fall chest.

this hunger is unprecedented.

this precise desire.

stretch your weariness against him.

let the water lap at
ankles like hungry flowers.

> when the moon tumbles,
> and morning cracks
> you open, you are ever alone again,
> evaporated, holding nothing,
> dreaming of sea anemones
> and belonging.

MEANTIME

while you

lose your face in altered states
mistaking situations like supermarkets in foreign places for outer
space

i

dance to the rhythm of your potential and rarefied brilliance
caress your discarded harp

ponder how i have nothing to offer
while giving you everything

across the vast expanse of the atlantic
it comes down to semantics

this frantic war of the words

you make me feel like i'm stealing something
when what i want is to hand over every last bit of me

and all i've got is nothing
but these penniless definitions
falling all over themselves
to get their two cents in

talk is cheap
nevertheless i go for broke

constructing worthless verses
which you belittle like inevitable destiny

it's not easy to battle with
an arsenal full of low self esteem

public defender
for inner criminal guilty as sin

you always win

listen
all i do is rise to fall

like boomerangs
orbiting planets
and dogs in heat
you always return to your point of entry
as predictable as 1before2before3

your oppressive weighs heavy
portentous like smallpox-soaked blankets
dangerous like its own omen

i crawl out from under your thumb
and end up backed against the wall
breathless and accused
i shake off the rain of your negativity
chilled to the bone
and i get wound up so tight
this massive mortal coil makes double helixes look relaxed and
loungey

and you
you make a better idea than human being
better in theory than practice

you
with your manic depressive passive aggressive propensity
to simultaneously create and avoid tension

you twist my intention like taffy
baffling me pink soft and harmless as baby-hand

you decide what i mean before i've even spoken

(son of mercilessly fucked with)

(we all got some walls up)
(it's understandable)

but i refuse to play stand-in for the role of your former assailant

this pulling
familiar taste of blood like sucking pennies
second nature in the mouth of a prizefighter

rearranging on the cellular level like metastasized panic

dancing with your deluge of demons like it takes two-hundred to tango

try to put me in my place

give me something to really struggle against

it's this genetic predilection towards rejection
i can not reason out this itch in my palms
or rhyme your name out of my dream-mantras
it is like vomit on my tongue now

it is a precarious position to be in

i am a daredevil
who dives headlong
eyes closed
wrists open
playing chicken with dignity
always braced for collision

P A R T S

behold how we
love like leprosy

different bits left behind

your forgotten harmonica on my bed stand and
my lips landing on your shoe

your unopened deodorant unnoticed for forty-eight hours
after you've flown and then
how you found my ear
pressed like prom corsage between the sheets of your journal

six separate times i find rusty belt studs
stuffed into the crack of my car seat and
one time while eating at that sidewalk café
my heart leapt straight out of my chest
she lay quivering and pulsating
on top of your pasta sauce

it was more than awkward
for both of us
as she indiscreetly begged you
to at least meet her halfway
and eat her out

little pieces of us
sprinkled like malignant fairy dust
about each others' consciousness

it's a singular dedication
loving like litterbugs

choosing our talismans
like shamans of dysfunction

then
letting them fly

like
bottlefuls of message

chucking chunks of self
like
it was nothing

like
a trail backwards

shedding everything

different bits left behind

like
there was something we
would eventually need
to re-
find
our way back to

after this particularly outstanding sacrifice

AND THIS IS THAT SHIFTING
IMPOSSIBLE PERSPECTIVE
THAT IS THE HUMAN CONDITION

lately,
when i close my eyes to sleep,
my dreams incarnate in variegated stages of invasion.
its amazing
the multiplicity of ways
the symbols instant replay:
my home overtaken by uninvited men
holding out handshakes full of agendas
and screenplays,
or i'm so close i can see the faces
of the snipers on the side of the freeway,
or doorless rooms, air heavy with the cool spun glass icicle satin
of fog clogging my lung passages with anthrax.
and does it really matter
that my stature
is completely out of hand
to
mouth existence?
and i am so far out of touch with my internal needs
that i can't even remember the feeling
of hungry?
for anything?
why scrutinize my own life
when it's all relative on the spectrum of perception?

> *and this is that shifting*
> *impossible perspective*
> *that is the human condition*

i reside (like we all do)
inside my own decided mythology.
i can say i failed completely at said intended eventuality,
or flip the script and simply claim that another path choose me.
both smack of insincerity,

leaving me liquefied,
more fluidity than history.
meaning, i can't, with any degree of certainty,
even give you a concrete map of what led me to this
righthererightnow.
terrified, trembling with
toomuchtruth,
all for you.
memory is as objective as the inconstant moon.
as a gaze at our own reflection
or an earful of our own vocal projection.

> *and this is that shifting*
> *impossible perspective*
> *that is the human condition*

we are inverted paradoxes,
inside-out stars,
with the light shining in,
contained in our skin.
sweet little packages of magic that can't unwrap themselves.
but i'm trying to, for me and you.
i'm trying to remind me and you that we are beautiful,
trying to confide in me and you
the realization that we can only ever truly be safe
in this temporary, luminous universe of helium balloons
and illusion.
we are human beings.
simply earthlings existing.
this mortal's coiled like childish livewire,
trying to unravel rapture,
delivering little scriptures
full of penniless potential.
filling fountains with thousands of wishes.
one c/sent to this planet with de facto struggles to overcome.
and even with all the differing degrees of lucidity surrounding me
we collectively agree, at the very least, that this is where we are
and this is when we be.
and even thinking that that doesn't mean anything
means something.

and i want to give you that single sentence
that gets you all sentient.
        and this is that shifting
i wish i could cull it down to a word or better yet, one letter
        impossible perspective
or even more so, just a moan, or less, an intake of breath, like...

...but you can never truly separate
        that is the human condition

                even subatomic particles
                change their behavior under our observation
                and here am i trying to capture life like butterflies

        and this is that shifting
        impossible perspective
        that is the human condition

                                        and i love you

CHOSEN

what if the clouds came in on me?
came in through the hole in my window screen?
sucked me clean out of here,
up to the stratosphere, where glitter-glue stars
that sparkle like tears would wrap me in
a sequin-
cloud-star-
fuzzy-warm-
blanket, softer than
the cumulonimbus from airplane windows appear?
and a black and magic silver winking me
would rise like a solar system christmas tree.
with planets for ornaments and stars for lights,
and i swallowed this image at the end of the night,
and the clouds that first found me returned me to my bed,
through the air, through the ozone,
(half naked, half dead,)
past the airplanes,
past the buildings,
past the seagulls that scream,
through the fissure that began it,
that rip in the screen.
and i took that sparkle with me,
'cause i'd swallowed it inside.
then i'd never be afraid,
and i'd never have to hide.
and i'd only have to give,
and i'd never have to take.
and nothing could ever really hurt me,
not asleep
or awake.
'cause it's all inconsequential
when around your neck hangs mars,
and you're loved,
and you're protected,
by one thousand
twinkling
stars.

SWEET CHILD

sweet child
the moment has arrived

great change waits at your doorstep
make way
it's time
to let *this little light* of yours *shine*
no wasting one second
guessing
be at the ready
be at the beck and call of the precipice of destiny
and then freefall into palpable culmination
trust that it's been leading up to this singularity
since the moment you entered existence

sweet child
the moment has arrived

rejoice recognize realize realign reconvene with your meaning
this is that reckoning
this is everything reacting to rapture
notice how even the air is alert
every breath so dedicated
and brimming with portent
that it catches itself
holds itself

all of nature on the verge or burgeoning bursting
flourishing with your bloom
tomatoes exploding with ripe on vines
tree bark so intense it peels with the crave of need
calla lilies bent over backwards
cats paused
paws poised mid-step
listening

sweet child
the moment has arrived

if you are still waiting for confirmation
let these words i speak right now be the final sign

you've been given symbols
with every flicker of those beautiful moonbeam eyes

sweet child
look and see

action is needed
this is what you were born for

brace yourself
by which i mean un-brace yourself
by which i mean become unbridled

sweet child
heed my call
gather your source material
you need it all
so you can use it all up inside
leave it all behind
like nothing experienced since or before
mop the floor with yourself
this is the *this* you've been waiting for

make way make ready make sure
alchemize yourself out of crude form today
you are divine
crack open your cocoon and shine

sweet child
the moment has arrived

RACHEL KANN

Rachel is the recipient of an L.A. Weekly Award and a
James Kirkwoood Award for Fiction. She's performed
her poetry at venues such as TEDx UCLA, Royce Hall,
Disney Concert Hall, California Plaza, The San Francisco
Palace of Fine Arts, and the Vans Warped Tour. Her writing
has appeared in various literary journals and anthologies
such as *Word Warriors* from Seal Press. Rachel lives in
Hollywood, California. Find her online at rachelkann.com

I am a sacred fug.

Made in the USA
Charleston, SC
07 July 2013